LIBRA
WITHDRAWN FR

KT-549-920

Welcome to…

The Hollywood Hills Clinic

*Where doctors to the stars
work miracles by day—
and explore their hearts' desires by night…*

When hotshot doc James Rothsberg started
the clinic six years ago he dreamed of a
world-class facility, catering to Hollywood's biggest
celebrities, and his team are unrivalled in their fields.
Now, as the glare of the media spotlight grows, the
Hollywood Hills Clinic is teaming up with the pro bono
Bright Hope Clinic, and James is reunited
with Dr Mila Brightman…the woman he jilted at the altar!

When it comes to juggling the care of Hollywood A-listers
with care for the underprivileged kids of LA *anything* can
happen…and sizzling passions run high in the shadow of
the red carpet. With everything at stake for James, Mila
and the Hollywood Hills Clinic medical team their biggest
challenges have only just begun!

Find out what happens in the dazzling

The Hollywood Hills Clinic miniseries:

Seduced by the Heart Surgeon
by Carol Marinelli

Falling for the Single Dad
by Emily Forbes

Tempted by Hollywood's Top Doc
by Louisa George

Perfect Rivals…
by Amy Ruttan

Look out for another four titles from
The Hollywood Hills Clinic over the next couple of months!

Dear Reader,

Thank you for picking up a copy of *Perfect Rivals…*! I can't believe this is my tenth book for Mills & Boon Medical Romance. It seems like only yesterday I sold my first book.

I was absolutely thrilled when the Medical team approached me about joining this continuity series—a series that is full of my favourite authors. I was excited and nervous at the same time.

Dr Florence Chiu is a character I instantly connected with. Her character absolutely gutted me repeatedly over the course of writing her story. I haven't had much experience in transplant surgery, but I know what an amazing gift donor organs can be, and for my heroine it means a second chance at life.

My hero is no stranger to Dr Chiu's world. He's lost someone very dear to him, and because of that he's guarded his heart and devoted his life to medicine. Having a fake relationship is the riskiest thing he's done in a long time.

I hope you enjoy Flo and Nate's story.

I love hearing from readers, so please drop by my website, amyruttan.com, or give me a shout on Twitter @ruttanamy.

With warmest wishes,

Amy Ruttan

PERFECT RIVALS…

BY
AMY RUTTAN

All rights reserved including the right of reproduction in whole or in part in any form. This edition is published by arrangement with Harlequin Books S.A.

This is a work of fiction. Names, characters, places, locations and incidents are purely fictional and bear no relationship to any real life individuals, living or dead, or to any actual places, business establishments, locations, events or incidents. Any resemblance is entirely coincidental.

This book is sold subject to the condition that it shall not, by way of trade or otherwise, be lent, resold, hired out or otherwise circulated without the prior consent of the publisher in any form of binding or cover other than that in which it is published and without a similar condition including this condition being imposed on the subsequent purchaser.

® and TM are trademarks owned and used by the trademark owner and/or its licensee. Trademarks marked with ® are registered with the United Kingdom Patent Office and/or the Office for Harmonisation in the Internal Market and in other countries.

Published in Great Britain 2016
By Mills & Boon, an imprint of HarperCollins*Publishers*
1 London Bridge Street, London, SE1 9GF

© 2016 Harlequin Books S.A.

Special thanks and acknowledgement are given to Amy Ruttan for her contribution to The Hollywood Hills Clinic *series.*

ISBN: 978-0-263-26425-8

Our policy is to use papers that are natural, renewable and recyclable products and made from wood grown in sustainable forests. The logging and manufacturing processes conform to the legal environmental regulations of the country of origin.

Printed and bound in Great Britain
by CPI Antony Rowe, Chippenham, Wiltshire

LIBRARIES NI

C900052267	
MAG	14.10.16
AF	£14.50
BAS	

Born and raised just outside Toronto, Canada, **Amy Ruttan** fled the big city to settle down with the country boy of her dreams. After the birth of her second child Amy was lucky enough to realise her lifelong dream of becoming a romance author. When she's not furiously typing away at her computer, she's mum to three wonderful children who use her as a personal taxi and chef.

Books by Amy Ruttan

Mills & Boon Medical Romance

Sealed by a Valentine's Kiss
His Shock Valentine's Proposal
Craving Her Ex-Army Doc

New York City Docs
One Night in New York

Safe in His Hands
Melting the Ice Queen's Heart
Pregnant with the Soldier's Son
Dare She Date Again?
It Happened in Vegas
Taming Her Navy Doc

Visit the Author Profile page at
millsandboon.co.uk for more titles.

This book is dedicated to my agent, Scott, for telling me to take this chance and write this continuity story.

Thank you to Elisa, who patiently answered my questions while I was researching this book. Thank you so much for all your help!

And a huge thank you to the Medical team for assigning me Flo and Nate's story. They were an amazing hero and heroine and I loved every second in their world.

**Praise for
Amy Ruttan**

'Amy Ruttan delivers an entertaining read that transports readers into a world of blissful romance set amidst the backdrop of the medical field. Sharp, witty and descriptive, *One Night in New York* is sure to keep readers turning the pages!'
—*Contemporary Romance Reviews*

'I highly recommend this for all fans of romance reads with amazing, absolutely breathtaking scenes, to-die-for dialogue, and everything else that is needed to make this a beyond awesome and *wow* read!'
—*Goodreads* on
Melting the Ice Queen's Heart

CHAPTER ONE

THIS TAKES ME BACK.

Dr. Flo Chiu remembered all the times she'd been raced to the hospital as a young girl. The familiar whir of a chopper coming in for a landing. Followed by the bump as the chopper landed, causing her to become nauseous. Even now, watching the helicopter, her stomach did a little flip. Everything reminded her of that moment. Something she hadn't thought about in a long time. The gray haze tinting the sky, as if it was promising rain, but this was Los Angeles. The haze was just smog. In Seattle, it would mean rain, and the day she'd flown in her own helicopter to a hospital helipad it had been raining.

Hard.

And that was all she remembered of her emergent helicopter ride over Seattle. That, and her father screaming out orders in Mandarin to a helicopter pilot who only spoke English, but, then, when her dad was frightened he often put aside his second language of English for his native tongue. And when her dad was mad, the beautiful language she loved to listen to was quick and hard to follow. It had frightened her to hear him talk like that.

She took a deep breath and wrapped her arms around herself, trying to shake the thought away. Usually she wasn't this nervous about another surgeon coming in to

The Hollywood Hills Clinic, but this was not just any other surgeon. This surgeon was her competition. This surgeon had been brought in specially from New York at the request of her patient. And her patient happened to be the world-famous, award-winning actor Kyle Francis. An actor she'd always admired and had had a bit of a crush on when she'd been fourteen.

She'd watched a lot of movies when she'd been younger. Of course, there hadn't been much else to do when you were confined to a hospital bed. And Kyle Francis had been the perfect twenty-something rising star and heartthrob of her youth.

On the outside Kyle had aged well. His heart and lungs, on the other hand, hadn't. Which was why he was now a patient.

He'd collapsed at a press conference in Los Angeles and had been brought straight to The Hollywood Hills Clinic, where it had quickly been established that Kyle Francis was dying.

And that's where Flo had stepped in.

She was, after all, a world-renowned transplant surgeon, and that's just what Kyle Francis needed. Actually, what he specifically needed was a heart and lung transplant.

It was right up Flo's alley. She'd done many, and on worse cases than Kyle, but if they let it go much longer, Kyle would be a worst-case scenario and it would make the job harder.

She had been wheeling Kyle into the operating room to help stabilize him until she had been stopped.

That was when Freya had dropped the bombshell on her that another surgeon was coming.

"Another surgeon? Why was another surgeon called,

Freya? I'm a damn good surgeon. I can do this surgery on my own. You've seen me do one."

"I know, but this is out of my hands, Flo. Mr. Francis's management team has called in Dr. King from Manhattan. Dr. King's the one who has been treating his failing heart and lungs for some time. There's no negotiation. You'll have to work with Dr. King."

Flo couldn't really argue with that.

So that's why she was here, huddled in the elevator, waiting for the helicopter to land and deposit this Dr. King in her lap. He was probably some old-money type of surgeon, and she only hoped that he would be willing to work with her. Some of these big-city surgeons were a pain in the rump to deal with. They didn't think someone who was only thirty had the skill to be an excellent or extraordinary surgeon and a transplant specialist to boot.

The chopper landed and Flo ducked down, holding back the wisps of black hair that were escaping from her long braid as she headed out onto the helipad to greet this new doctor.

Please, don't be a jerk. Please, don't be a jerk.

She could deal with almost anyone but a jerk. Other surgeons tended to look down on her because of her size and her gender. That, and she looked a lot younger than her age. Even though she hoped this surgeon wasn't a jerk, she'd been warned about his arrogance so she braced herself for it.

The door of the chopper opened and her mouth almost dropped open in surprise. Dr. King was not at all what she had expected. He wasn't old at all. Probably in his mid-thirties. Tall, tanned and muscular. His blond hair was tousled and short. His face was chiseled, and the well-tailored gray suit molded his broad chest and thick muscular thighs almost perfectly. He was an all-

American high-school hottie. The kind of man who had probably got through med school on a football scholarship. The kind of man who would have ignored a perpetually sick, geeky wallflower like her at school dances. The kind of man she'd always secretly wished would look her way.

Johnny had been good looking, but not like this, and look how that had turned out. Flo shook her ex from her thoughts. He'd been gone for a long time and there was no place for him in her mind today.

Heat rushed to her cheeks when he turned to look at her. Light blue, almost ice-blue eyes fixed their hard gaze on her, as if assessing her and sizing her up in a matter of moments. It unnerved her, but also excited her. She almost wondered what it would be like steal a kiss from a man like this. And then she kicked herself mentally for thinking about the competition this way.

No matter how attractive she thought he was, he was still the competition.

All-American athletes like him were the kind of guy she'd always wanted to date. At least once in her life, because it wasn't the type of guy her father or mother would like if she brought him home. They hadn't been thrilled with Johnny either and he was a lawyer.

Focus. He's staring at you.

It was then she realized the chopper had already left the helipad and was headed away from the clinic toward LAX.

"Are you all right?" he asked.

"Fine. Dr. King, I'm—"

"I don't have time for pleasantries. You need to take me to my patient."

Great. He's a pompous jerk.

Well, an arrogant surgeon she could deal with. Her

father was an arrogant businessman in Beijing and Se-attle. Flo's mother, who was American, was the only one who could get him to toe the line, and she'd taught Flo well. She'd taught her not to cower to arrogant men and to stand up for herself. Especially in light of the fact that Flo had been sick her whole life and people tried to walk all over her.

"As I was saying, I'm Dr. Chiu and I'm head of trans-plant surgery here at The Hollywood Hills Clinic. I've been treating Mr. Francis since his collapse last night."

Dr. King's eyes widened in shock. "Is that so?"

"Yes. Now, if you will follow me, Dr. King, I will take you to *our* patient." She got into the elevator and when he also entered, she pushed the button for the wing that housed Kyle Francis. It was the wing that had the most security to guarantee privacy for high-profile patients.

"Did you say 'our' patient, Dr. Chiu?"

"I did."

"I have to say I'm a bit confused. Kyle Francis has been my patient for a couple of years now. I'm the one who put him on the transplant list. He's my patient."

She grinned at him sardonically. "Oh, no. He's *our* pa-tient. Mr. Francis's management team may have flown you in here, but the transplant wing is my wing. I'm granting you surgical privileges here, buster, and don't you forget it."

He grinned at her, amused, or at least she hoped so as those ice-blue eyes were twinkling. "Buster? I've never heard that one before."

Flo rolled her eyes, but smiled. "Sorry. Something I picked up from my mother."

The elevator doors opened up and Flo swiped her se-curity card to open the doors to allow them entry to the high-security wing. Kyle's large suite was at the end of the hall.

"So, when he arrived he was bradycardic. We got his breathing and rhythm stabilized, but it's apparent to me that his heart is failing and his time is running out. He needs to be put on a left ventricular assist device."

"An LVAD?" Dr. King nodded. "I can see why you would think that, but let's not jump to conclusions. We don't know what caused the collapse. He was stable when he left New York last week. And putting him on a left ventricular assist device complicates his transplant further."

"I am aware of that. I'm not jumping to conclusions. I've performed a heart and lung transplant before, Dr. King. I know what I'm doing. I know what I'm seeing."

"Then if you know what it is, why isn't he on a left ventricular assist device?"

Really?

"I was about to have him prepped for the OR when his management team put a stop to the procedure and insisted on flying you out here, Dr. King."

"Nate."

"Pardon?" Flo said as she picked up a tablet to bring up Kyle's chart.

"My name is Nathaniel, but you can call me Nate. And what can I call you, Dr. Chiu?"

"You can call me Dr. Chiu." She tried to step past him, but he blocked her path.

"If you knew my patient, you would know that he likes everything to be informal. It puts him at ease. So I think it's in the best interests of the patient that we address each other by our given names."

"My name is Florence, but everyone calls me Flo." She handed him the tablet with Kyle's chart.

He grinned. "Thank you, Flo. Let's see *our* patient, shall we?"

Flo gritted her teeth. This was going to be a trying ordeal and it had nothing to do with the complicated surgery that awaited Kyle Francis. Someone was going to die and it wouldn't be the patient if Dr. Nate King kept being a thorn in her side.

Nate didn't particularly want to be back in California, even though he'd grown up here and his parents now lived up in San Francisco. He hadn't been back to California since he'd started medical school, and that had been years ago.

He hadn't been in California since the accident. Since Serena had died when they'd been rock climbing on El Capitan in Yosemite National Park. He just couldn't be in the place where they'd fallen in love, the place where they'd lived for the rush, whether it had been surfing breakers in the Pacific Ocean, skiing at Mammoth Mountain or rock climbing.

Serena had been an adrenaline junkie, just like him.

And then, on a climb they'd done a hundred times before, a rope had given way and Serena had fallen.

His guilt still ate at him. He was so certain he'd checked all those clips, tightened the rope, but he couldn't recall actually doing it and her death weighed on him.

He'd realized then how recklessly he'd been living. So he'd taken the scholarship at Harvard and thrown himself into schooling. Nate had sworn over Serena's coffin that he would become the best damn transplant surgeon, focusing a lot of his research on regeneration and the means to sustain life longer when there were no viable donors.

People died every day while they waited on the transplant list.

Serena had died while she'd waited.

Don't think about her now.

Nate stared at the chart, at the scans they'd done on Kyle when he'd been admitted to The Hollywood Hills Clinic.

Dang. She was right.

Kyle needed a left ventricular assist device and he needed one right away. She was watching him as he scanned Kyle's chart. He snuck a glance, just a brief glance, at her and he tried not to smile. He didn't want to give her an inch.

She was feisty. There was a certain passion hidden deep in that petite frame. Her skin was almost flawless and her long black hair shone in the tight braid down her back, except for the few stray wisps that floated around her perfect oval face. Her eyes were dark brown, like chocolate, and they glinted as she watched him. Her full ruby lips were pressed together firmly, as if she was waiting for the moment to smirk at him when he announced that she'd been right.

Dr. Florence Chiu was intelligent, gorgeous and full of life. She didn't back down from him, even though he towered over her five-foot-five frame at six feet.

If he hadn't sworn off the idea of women in general, he would pursue a woman just like Dr. Chiu. He liked a bit of wildness as well as the fact she was a transplant surgeon. It was as if she was the perfect woman for him.

Don't think about her like that.

Just from a quick moment in Flo's presence he realized that she was a danger to his well-being. He was not looking for love.

He'd been hurt before. His heart had shattered when Serena had died, so Flo was off-limits. He was here to work. He was here for his patient and that's all that mattered. Being the foremost transplant surgeon on the east coast afforded him the ability to further his research on finding other means of sustaining organs or life while patients waited for organs.

All that mattered to Nate was his career and he had to remember that. Love was not for him. He didn't deserve it.

He cleared his throat. "You're right, Dr. Chiu. He does need a left ventricular assist device. I assume, since you were prepping for surgery, that you have one ready to go?"

Flo nodded. "Yes. I can prep the OR in about an hour and we can get him in there and hooked up to the equipment. I'm sorry that your trip to California was a waste."

He cocked his head to one side and smiled at her. "Why is it a waste now?"

"Well, clearly I can handle this here. You came here and basically said I was right in the course of my treatment for Mr. Francis, so you can go back to New York."

Such tenacity.

"Oh, Dr. Chiu. I'm not heading anywhere. Mr. Francis is my top priority. There are other surgeons in New York who can run my service while I'm here. I'm staying and I plan to be in that OR with you and assist you in implanting the LVAD."

"You're kidding, right?"

"No. I never kid when it comes to my patients. I have been treating Mr. Francis for a couple of years. I'm the one who put him on the transplant list and I'll be the one performing his transplant, even if that means I'll be spending years in California. I'm not leaving his side."

Her mouth had opened to say something else when alarms went off and a code blue was called in Kyle's suite. They ran into the suite and a nursing team was already working over him.

"He's crashing, Dr. Chiu!" Nurse Olivia Dempsey called out as she lowered the bed and the rest of the team rushed in with an AED and tray of instruments.

Flo jumped into action, rapidly firing off instructions as Kyle Francis flatlined. Nate wasn't leaving his patient.

He wasn't going anywhere. Even if it meant staying in California. Even if it meant being tempted constantly by Dr. Chiu. He was made of strong mettle. He could resist temptation.

Couldn't he?

CHAPTER TWO

DON'T DIE. DON'T DIE.

Flo glanced up at the monitors as she worked on Kyle Francis, and she tried not to think about the fact that Dr. Nate King was standing on the opposite side of the bed, working with her as they tried to stabilize him. If Kyle died, he'd judge her. He seemed like the arrogant type who would put the blame on her when really it was the management team that Kyle employed who would be at fault. They were the ones who'd put a stop to her helping him right away, insisting that Dr. King be flown in.

Making her and Kyle wait.

That wouldn't have happened if she'd been allowed to put in the left ventricular assist device when Kyle had first come in, and she was going to make sure that Freya and James Rothsberg both knew that. Especially if Kyle died.

Come on.

Right now she'd like to throttle that acting management team. Their delay might've cost Kyle his life.

"Come on," she whispered under her breath as she pictured all the thousand ways she'd torture Kyle's managers.

There was a bleep from the monitor as the sensor picked up a faint pulse. Flo gave an inward sigh of relief. Thoughts of murder and disemboweling some Hollywood yuppies dissipating for now.

"Good job, everyone!" She took off her latex gloves as the nursing team stepped in to make sure that Kyle didn't code again. "I need this man prepped and ready for surgery. I'm on my way to get an OR prepped. I want a repeat of his labs drawn."

"Yes, Dr. Chiu," said Olivia.

"Make sure that I'm informed of those labs as well, Nurse," Nate said, not even glancing in the direction of Flo's favorite transplant nurse.

Olivia looked at Flo for confirmation and she nodded.

Flo glanced at Nate, who was scowling as he monitored Kyle's vitals. She thought maybe she could sneak past him. She didn't want to deal with arrogance this minute. Moments like that just brought back the vivid memories of the time she'd collapsed during band practice. When her kidney had failed her at fourteen and she had been rushed to hospital.

They were jumbled memories, but her parents liked to tell that story about how she'd hovered near death. She'd needed a donor then and Kyle needed one now. But a heart and lung transplant match was tricky. The list was long and the United Network of Organ Sharing didn't care who Kyle was. Placement on the list was prioritized on who got on the list first.

There were other people waiting for a heart and lung transplant. Kyle was at the top of two lists, one for the heart and one for the lungs. He had to have both at the same time from the same donor.

At least the left ventricular assist device would stabilize Kyle while they waited. By the time her kidney had failed, dialysis had no longer worked for her. At least kidneys could be donated by a living donor.

You could live with one kidney.

Flo always had.

Her stomach twisted as she thought of that, because her time was so uncertain. She'd had this kidney for fifteen years now. How much longer until she was on her sickbed? On dialysis and waiting for another transplant?

Another precious gift so she could go on living?

Which was why she had to continue to live life to the fullest.

"Going somewhere, Dr. Chiu?"

Drat.

She turned around to see that Nate had followed her out of Kyle's suite. "I'm going to schedule our surgery."

"I'm so glad you said 'our' surgery."

Flo rolled her eyes and he fell into step beside her. "Really, I can handle this surgery on my own."

"I know you can, but what would be the fun in that?" Nate asked, his scowl changing into a teasing smile.

"Trust me. It's fun." She grinned back at him and he chuckled. He had a gorgeous smile, perfect white teeth against that tanned face. There was a faint scar that ran through his eyebrow and another on his chin.

Definitely a jock.

"So where can I get set up with a pager and scrubs? I wouldn't mind an office, either."

"You're not asking for much, are you?" Flo remarked.

"Well, if I'm going to be here a while I would like to continue my research."

"Research? What're you researching or is that a secret?"

"No. It's no secret. I've published several papers on regenerative tissues as well as robotic and mechanical devices to prolong organs and life while waiting for transplants."

Flo was impressed. She'd never read any of Nate's papers, but the premise was interesting.

"Well, if you're looking for a place to set up shop then you would have to talk to Freya Rothsberg, but she's gone home for the evening."

"Okay, I'll talk to her in the morning. I don't have to talk to her about getting a pair of scrubs, do I?"

Flo laughed. She couldn't help it. The jerk was charming. She pointed to the OR charge desk, where a nurse sat behind her desk and was electronically entering patients' details onto a vast surgical board. "No, just speak to that OR nurse and she'll point you in the right direction."

He smiled again, one that made her melt just slightly, before he headed off to get scrubs. She admired his well-defined backside as he strode away.

Don't think about him like that.

Flo had no time for romantic inclinations, because the one time she had and Johnny had found out that she had a chronic kidney disease because of her time in NICU, he'd run in the opposite direction, breaking her heart. He had crushed her completely. It was easier to guard her heart than have it mangled by someone you thought you loved and who loved you back. She'd bared her most intimate side to Johnny, but the moment he'd seen her scar, the game had changed. Attraction had been replaced by disgust and fear. Even pity.

So Flo had given up on the notion of love. Which was probably why she was still a virgin at thirty.

She didn't need it. Besides, if she involved someone else in her life they would tell her that her bucket list was crazy and no one was going to dictate to her how she was going to live her life. She'd been given a gift when she'd been given that kidney and she wasn't going to spend the rest of her life like she'd spent her childhood, wrapped up in cotton wool by two well-meaning but overprotective parents.

No, she was going to live her life to the fullest, until her donor kidney failed and she'd go back on the list again. When she was waiting she'd have all these amazing memories to think about and not have any regrets if she died while on the list.

And no man was going to get in her way.

Not even the all-American hottie she had always pined for.

"Suction, please," Flo said.

"With pleasure." Nate suctioned around the area where Flo was working. Usually he was the one giving directions about suctioning or retracting, but instead he was the one on the other side of the table from the lead surgeon and it made him grind his teeth just a bit.

At least Flo had let him into her OR, because she was correct—she had every right to tell him to take off. She was the head of transplant surgery, he was just the patient's doctor from out east. Nate was very aware that he was in Dr. Flo Chiu's territory.

Scrub nurses and residents alike all respected and admired Dr. Chiu. Even though he should be bitter about the fact that she was working on his patient, he couldn't help but admire her surgical skill. Her tiny, delicate hands handled the heart with precision as she carefully sutured in the device. A device that would allow Kyle to live a bit longer.

"It's amazing how this can sustain his life," Nate remarked.

"Yes. It is. Medical research such as yours, Dr. King, is definitely valuable."

"You know, for a long time LVADs couldn't be used on children or women."

"I know, Dr. King."

"I know you do, Dr. Chiu, but maybe some of your residents in this room can tell me why LVADs couldn't be used on women and children in the past."

Flo shot him a look. "There are no residents here. The Hollywood Hills Clinic isn't a teaching hospital. All these surgeons are transplant fellows."

"Well, a fellow still has to learn under a seasoned surgeon." Nate glanced around the room. "Come on, someone has to know the answer."

"Would someone answer Dr. King, please? And maybe after this Dr. King would stop subjecting us to his pub quiz on cardiothoracic surgery."

There was laughter and Nate had to laugh to himself, as well.

Oh, she's feisty.

He liked that in a woman. Strong and not afraid to stand up for herself.

Flo wasn't afraid of much.

"The LVAD device was too large for the chests of women and children, that's why it couldn't be used on them in the past," a surgeon finally said.

"Right, thank you." Nate turned back to Flo. "See, this is why I'm doing my research and maybe this young doctor here would like to assist me while I continue with my research here in Los Angeles."

"Thank you, Dr. King," the surgeon said, stunned.

Flo shot him another look that said, *Are you kidding me?*

"I never questioned why you were doing your research, Dr. King. I admire it, but since Mr. Francis here will be stabilized, albeit bound to this hospital with his LVAD, maybe you could return to New York. I'll let you know when UNOS has a heart and lung ready for Mr. Francis." Flo continued with her work.

"Ah, but that's the thing. They won't be calling you, Dr. Chiu. UNOS will call me. I'm the one who put Mr. Francis on the transplant list."

Her head snapped back up and she fixed him with a stern look over her surgical mask.

That got her attention.

"You are persistent in your need to stay here, aren't you?" she said, with a hint of admiration in her voice.

"When it comes to my patients I am very persistent."

She looked up at him briefly and he knew by the way her eyes crinkled in the corners that she was smiling behind that mask. "Me, too."

"Dr. Chiu, I don't see why we both can't work together on Mr. Francis's care. We don't both have to stay at this hospital twenty-four-seven, waiting for a heart and lungs. Surely you have a life outside this hospital?"

"What're you implying, Dr. King? Are you implying I don't have a life?"

"On the contrary, I'm sure you have a life. Someone special."

"What?" she asked, not looking at him.

"A boyfriend."

There were a few titters in the crowd and Flo quickly shot them all a dirty look, which silenced the laughter.

"Not that it's any of your business, Dr. King, but I don't have a boyfriend. My work is my life."

"Oh, that's a shame."

Flo groaned. "Don't tell me you're one of those kinds of men?"

"What kind of men?"

"Men who think that a woman is worthless if she doesn't have a boyfriend or a significant other."

"No, I'm not. It's just…" Then he trailed off as he thought about Serena. "Life's too short."

She looked up at him, her brown eyes warm and tender as if silently agreeing with him. As if she knew personally how fragile life was, and he couldn't help but wonder what had happened in her life. Had she lost someone she'd cared about?

Nate certainly hoped not. That was a pain he wouldn't wish on his worst enemy.

"You're right," she said. "Life is too short. At least with this operation he won't be one of the ten to fifteen percent who die while waiting. It will give him a chance to beat the odds."

Nate nodded, but didn't say anything further as they worked together to attach Kyle's left ventricular assist device. Kyle was lucky that they'd brought him to Dr. Chiu, in light of the fact that he himself was based in New York.

There was talent here.

There was skill.

Together they could save Kyle's life. There were always variables when it came to heart and lung transplants, but maybe together they could succeed.

No. You can't. Not together.

Flo was the type of woman his old self would have pursued in a heartbeat and that thought scared him. If he had to work closely with her, then he would be tempted.

How could he not be tempted by a woman like Flo?

He had to keep his distance from her. It would be hard, but he had to put a wall between the two of them. It had to be professional. It had to be businesslike. That was all there was to it. Nate couldn't risk his heart again.

Risk was a dangerous thing and he wasn't willing to play around with that.

Look where his life of risk had gotten him.

Don't think about Serena now. You don't deserve to mourn her.

After the surgery was successfully completed, Nate didn't say much. He just scrubbed out and then tried to find his way off the surgical floor. He needed air. It took him a few minutes, but he found his way back up to the roof, to the helipad. Maybe the height would get him out of the LA smog.

It was hot out, different from New York, where the bitter remnants of March still clung to the city. He'd forgotten how much he missed the heat of California. He took a deep breath and tried to calm his jangled nerves.

He couldn't remember the last time he'd felt like this.

Since Serena had died he'd been busy burying his feelings in his work. He didn't usually connect with anyone, but Flo had got under his skin.

Even in the brief time he'd known her.

She made him forget. She made him forget how he had a tight rein on his emotions. Absolute control at all times.

"There you are," Flo said behind him, making him jump slightly.

"Why did you follow me up here?" he snapped.

"Don't get so testy. I followed you because I wanted to give you this temporary pass." She held out the scan card in her delicate fingers. "If you don't have this you can't get access to Mr. Francis or basically get around the hospital."

Nate sighed inwardly and took the scan card from her. "Sorry. Thanks."

"I guess I could've kept it and you would've been trapped up here." A smile played at the corners of her lips. "You would deserve it, too, asking all those personal questions during surgery. My team doesn't need to know about my personal life."

"I was trying to lighten the mood in there."

Since when?

In New York City he was always serious. Residents and interns alike quaked in their boots around him. He wasn't known for lightening the mood, or even chatting in an operating room. He didn't know what had come over him.

She crossed her arms. "There was no need for mood lightening in there. Besides, from what I hear, you're not exactly jovial all the time."

"Who told you that?" he asked.

"Mr. Francis, when he first came in and was stabilized. When he found out his management team had called you he warned me about you. He said you were a bit of an arrogant brute."

"I doubt he said arrogant brute."

"You're right," she said, a twinkle in her eyes. "It was much more colorful."

Nate chuckled to himself. That sounded like something Kyle would do. And when he glanced at Flo he could see a soft side to her. She gave off the appearance of being a tough cookie in the operating room, but there was a softness about her. A warmth.

Something he'd been missing in his life for so long.

"Thanks for helping me in there. I'm so glad he's stabilized. Let's just hope we can keep him that way until UNOS calls *you*." She smiled at him. "I'll leave you to it. If you need anything, just have me paged. I'll be at the hospital for some time still."

She turned to leave, but Nate reached out and took her elbow to stop her. Flo turned, a questioning look on her face.

"Thank you for being here to help my patient," he said. "I'm glad a surgeon of your caliber was here to help him. And I'll get UNOS to add you to the call list."

Her brown eyes widened in surprise and then she smiled, a pink blush tinging her round cheeks as she tucked an errant wisp of hair behind her ear. "Thank you, and of course."

Nate knew that he should let her go, only he couldn't. He felt mesmerized by her and without thinking he pulled her tight against and kissed her.

For one moment, while he tasted her sweet lips, he felt her melt against him, which prompted him to wrap his arms around her, deepening the kiss. Her petite body was pressed against his, his hands in her hair as he bent over to kiss her.

Nate wanted to take this further. If they had been back at his place in New York, he'd be scooping her up in his arms and carrying her off to bed to make love to her, but he was standing with her on a helipad in Los Angeles.

He was tumbling down a dangerous path.

Then he remembered what he was doing.

That this was not keeping his distance from her at all. It was the exact opposite.

He broke off the kiss and took a step away from her, running his hand through his hair, trying to calm the erratic beat of his pulse and the longing in his blood.

Flo stood there, just as shocked as he was, her fingers pressing her lips, her eyes wide.

"I'm sorry. I don't know…" He trailed off. He knew what had come over him and he was angry at himself for letting lust take over his senses, even for just one moment.

"No, it's okay," she said quickly. "The rush of the moment. I get it. We won't talk about it again, Dr. King."

And then, before he had a chance to say anything else, she turned on her heel and jogged away, putting the distance between them that he should've done in the first place.

CHAPTER THREE

FLO WOKE WITH a start and forgot for a moment that she was in an on-call room. Her arm had pins and needles because when she'd crashed, she'd crashed with her arm hanging over the side of the bed, clutching her pager, which was currently vibrating in her hand.

She glanced at it and saw that Freya Rothsberg was looking for her.

Drat.

She hoped it didn't have anything to do with sharing her office with Nate. She wouldn't have really minded or put up a fight before, but after yesterday Flo knew that sharing an office was a *bad* idea.

She'd been so surprised when he'd pulled her into his strong arms and kissed her. A little voice inside her head had told her to push him away, but she'd been unable to because the kiss had been the hottest kiss she'd ever had.

Every other kiss in her life, before Nate's kiss, had been chaste in comparison. The moment his hand had cupped the back of her head, his fingers playing in the wisps of hair at the back of her neck, it had sent a jolt of pure longing and desire through her veins.

And she'd wanted him.

That side of her that lived for the moment had screamed at her to take him. Though the sensible side of her had reminded her that the last time she'd become close to a man, when she'd almost taken the plunge and had had sex, a certain scar had scared Johnny. It spoke to the world that she was ill. That her life was uncertain, and no one wanted to be tied down to a risk. Johnny had made that much clear.

He'd been afraid to touch her again after he'd seen the scar, and she'd told him why she had it hoping that would calm the issue, but it hadn't. It had just made it worse. Besides, what did she really know about sex? She'd never had it before.

It was good that Nate had broken off that kiss, though it was going to be hard to work with him. Especially if Freya insisted that they share an office.

Flo got out of bed, tidied her hair and brushed her teeth in the on-call room, then made her way to her office. Thankfully, her administrative assistant wasn't in yet, because Sally would certainly pepper her with a ton of questions about Kyle Francis and Flo's bedraggled appearance.

You slept in the on-call room again, didn't you?

Flo locked the door to her office and went to the closet to pull out the set of business clothes that she always kept on hand, because this wasn't the first time she'd slept over at The Hollywood Hills Clinic and had needed to make an appearance in front of the bosses the next day.

She tossed her scrubs in the laundry basket and then pulled on a reliable white blouse and pinstripe black pencil skirt. She traded her comfortable running shoes for her black heels and hoped no one would see the dents in her ankles from the elastic in her socks after wearing them all night.

Flo fixed her hair, putting it up in a bun, and then slipped on her white lab coat, attaching her security cards and identification. With one last look she reached down and grabbed a tablet so she could bring up Kyle Francis's file, because she was positive that Freya would want to talk about that.

Once she had everything she quickly made her way through the halls of The Hollywood Hills Clinic to the boardroom, where Freya had asked her to meet her, which also had Flo's nerves on edge. She knocked and then entered the boardroom and tried not to blush when she saw Nate sitting in a chair at the table.

He was chatting to Freya amicably, but the moment Flo walked in those piercing blue eyes trained on her, and it took all her willpower to stop her knees knocking together. She would not let Nate get to her.

They were colleagues. That's it.

Besides, even if something came of it, once he found out she was a transplant patient herself, he'd run, like all the others had. Her uncertain future like kryptonite to men. Which was why she kept it to herself, both in her personal and professional life.

"Sorry for running late, Freya."

"No, it's quite all right, Flo. Please have a seat." Freya motioned to the seat directly across from Nate, on her left side. Flo sat down and tried not to look in Nate's direction.

"I understand Mr. Francis has been stabilized?" Freya said, sitting down at the head of the table and brushing her long hair over her shoulder in that refined way she had.

"He has." Flo pulled up Kyle's file. "The surgical report is here if you need it."

Freya held up her hand. "No, I'm not here to talk about Mr. Francis's surgery. I'm glad to know that he's been stabilized."

"I thought you wanted to talk about Kyle Francis? The page said there was going to be discussion about him."

"Well, it's indirectly about Mr. Francis." Freya brought up an image on the screen behind her with a click of the remote.

Flo almost fell out of her chair when she saw the headline of a local paper and the photograph that was underneath it.

Superstar Kyle Francis's doctors locked in a kiss while actor hovers near death.

"And then there's this one." Freya clicked the remote again and a close-up photograph of Flo in Nate's arms, lips locked, was emblazoned across a more reputable local paper with the caption underneath, *Love match between heart surgeons.*

"We're not heart surgeons," Nate joked, trying to defuse the situation. "We have cardiothoracic training, but we only transplant hearts when it comes to cardio care."

Freya fixed her sternest gaze on him. "Yet the world knows Kyle Francis is waiting for a heart and lung transplant."

"How did they know that?"

Freya sighed, "A paramedic leaked it. Not someone from our clinic thankfully, but still security and privacy measures at our clinic are now being questioned. Especially in light of a paramedic leaking the information about Kyle Francis's surgery and then a paparazzo snapping a picture of two surgeons making out on the roof of our clinic. Our reputation is on the line."

Flo's stomach twisted in a knot and she felt like she was going to be sick.

How could she have been so foolish? She liked to

live for the moment and take risks, but not when it jeopardized her career or the reputation of The Hollywood Hills Clinic.

"Freya, I'm so sorry..."

"There's no need to apologize, Flo. There's still a chance to solve this problem." She smiled at them both. "Which is why I'm so glad both of you are dressed respectably. We're going to hold a press conference in a few moments."

"A press conference about what?" Nate asked.

"We're going to talk about Kyle's procedure. We have clearance from his management team. It will be good PR for him. We're also going to talk about a pro bono case that both of you will be working on. We'll be working in conjunction with the Bright Hope Clinic to help Eva Martinez. She's a child in need of a kidney transplant. Her mother, a single mom and waitress, is a perfect match and is donating a kidney to her daughter. It's caught the attention of the media."

Flo's heart skipped a beat as Freya brought up the dossier of Eva Martinez. Eva was twelve. Just a couple of years younger than she herself had been when she'd needed her kidney transplant. It struck a chord deep in her heart.

"Of course," Flo said, finally finding her voice. "Of course I'm willing to work on a pro bono case for a child. That's no problem."

"Is that all?" Nate asked.

"No," Freya said quietly, crossing her arms and leaning back in the chair. "We have to address the issue of two prominent transplant surgeons kissing on the roof of The Hollywood Hills Clinic and being caught doing it."

"There's nothing between us," Flo said quickly. "It won't happen again."

Nate was eyeing her speculatively, as if she'd slapped him or something. "Of course. It won't happen again. It was an impulse after a long surgery."

"I don't need to know why it happened. I don't care if our surgeons date, but I do care about the fact those two surgeons were caught kissing on the clinic roof when we advertise privacy and security to our VIPs. So, I want you two to pretend you're in a relationship."

Flo blinked, because she couldn't believe what Freya was saying. "Pardon?"

"The Hollywood Hills dream team is going to save the life of Eva Martinez *and* Kyle Francis. The positive PR this will bring to The Hills is too good an opportunity to pass up. We need to restore our reputation. Until that reputation is restored and our clients begin to trust us again, your wagons are officially hitched together."

Nate knew he should refuse, get up and walk away. After all, he wasn't a surgeon at the clinic. He was only here because of his patient and that's why he couldn't leave.

He also didn't want to hurt Flo.

She was a surgeon here at The Hollywood Hills Clinic. Her reputation would be tainted because of this. He really didn't have much of choice. He might not like it, but it was just a prettiness. It wasn't like they had to *do* anything, and he didn't have plans to surf the local single scene in California. It wasn't going to put a damper on his style.

"Okay," Nate said.

"Okay?" Flo asked, shocked, and she fixed him with an *are you crazy* look.

"I'm fine with the pretense and I'm more than happy to help that little girl. The fact that a match has already been found makes it all the easier. I don't mind working on a pro bono case."

Freya smiled. "Good. What about you, Flo?"

Flo was sitting back in her chair, still in shock. "I guess that's okay. I'm fine with the pro bono case and… yeah, I'm fine with the other angle."

"Good," Freya said, and stood. "I'll let the press into the press room and we'll get this conference started in ten minutes."

Nate watched as Freya walked out of the boardroom, leaving Flo and him by themselves. They didn't say anything to each other. There was lots he wanted to say to Flo; he wanted to apologize to her, because it was his fault they were in this situation. He was the one who'd been unable to control his desire for her.

He'd acted impetuously. Something he hadn't done in a long time.

This is why I need to maintain control and keep my distance at all times.

If he didn't maintain that tight control on himself, he acted irrationally and people paid for his indiscretion. Which was why he always tried to remain in control. Control of his life was the most important thing.

"Well, perhaps we should get to the press room."

"What was that?" Flo asked, her arms crossed.

"What was what?" he asked.

"Why did you agree so easily? I thought you would've put up a fight. I mean, you don't work for the clinic. You could just leave, go back to New York."

Nate snorted. "You'd like that, wouldn't you?"

Flo rolled her eyes. "This doesn't have anything to do with Kyle's surgery."

"Doesn't it?" Nate stood and leaned over the board-room table. "You've been trying to get me to go back home since I first arrived. You don't like another surgeon sniffing around your territory."

Flo grinned. "You're right. I don't, but I had resigned myself to the fact you were staying. Honestly, if it were my patient I would probably do the same thing. What I don't understand now is why you're being so accommodating."

"Look, it was my fault what happened up there. I shouldn't have done it. I was an idiot and not thinking clearly. If I could go back in time and change the fact that I kissed you I would. It was a huge mistake."

A faint trace of disappointment crossed her face. "Okay."

"Let's just put on our best professional facades out there and play nice. Besides, I look forward to working on a kidney transplant with you. It should be a simple surgery."

A strange look passed over her face again, one he couldn't recognize as other than pain, but it was just fleeting as she stood up and straightened her lab coat. "Right. A nice pro bono case. Good PR."

There was a hint of bitterness to her tone.

"Are you okay?" Nate asked.

"Now you care how I feel?" Flo asked.

"Well, I am supposed to be your boyfriend. I might as well get into the act."

Flo shook her head and sighed. "Come on, then, Mr. Dreamboat. Let's get this press conference over with."

"That's Dr. Dreamboat to you," Nate teased.

Flo stuck out her tongue and they walked out of the boardroom and headed toward the press conference, with a lot of gazes fixed on them. A few whispers. So word had got out already about the "dream team".

Nate took Flo's hand and she flinched, so he leaned over, the scent of her soap tickling his senses.

"Relax, we're supposed to hold hands. We're a couple."

Flo nodded and then held her head high as they walked hand in hand to the press conference. Though he shouldn't like it, he did. Her delicate hands, the ones that had so expertly stitched in that left ventricular assist device just yesterday, were strong and soft in his.

And it felt right.

Too right.

The moment they stepped into the press conference they were met by a ton of flashes and questions being fired at them. Flo looked a bit shell shocked. Perhaps she wasn't used to press conferences, but Nate was.

He often spoke to the board and at conferences about transplant surgery. This was an old hat for him. The only thing that was a bit new for him, and unwelcome at that, was pretending to be Flo's significant other.

Well, it wasn't totally unwelcome to pretend to be Flo's boyfriend. What bothered him was that he wanted to act on it. He wanted another kiss. All the previous night in his hotel he'd thought about her, to the point he'd been unable to sleep and had spent most of the night in the hotel's swimming pool, swimming laps to burn off energy.

Energy that he'd wanted to spend in a different way.

Don't think about it.

"It's okay," Nate whispered in her ear, reassuringly. "Just smile. This is for The Hollywood Hills Clinic, remember?"

"Right," Flo said through gritted teeth, and she nodded as they made their way to the podium, taking a seat on either side of Freya.

He could do this. Keep his cool.

He could go with this charade.

He was made of strong mettle.

This was just an act. Just a risky, foolish act. One he should be keeping far away from.

CHAPTER FOUR

FLO'S PULSE THUNDERED in her ears. She didn't like crowds too much. Crowds like this just reminded her of junior high school when she'd been a sickly girl sitting off on the sidelines but wanting to be part of the action. Her mom had taught her to be strong, but that was usually in a one-on-one situation. There were a lot of people in this room. People who weren't doctors.

Stand her in front of a bunch of other surgeons, doctors and nurses in a conference setting and she was fine. Press? That was new territory. Especially given the fact that she was on the arm of the hottest man in the room.

And usually good-looking men didn't get to her, either. James Rothsberg was in the room and Flo had always found him attractive, with his golden blond hair, deep blue eyes and athletic frame. So what was it about Dr. Nathaniel King that made her feel so nervous?

Probably because you've never kissed James Rothsberg and have no desire to do so.

Whereas Nate King. Oh, yeah, she'd been fighting that craving since he'd first got off the helicopter.

Get a grip on yourself.

Freya was talking, but Flo really couldn't focus on what she was saying. She was talking about The Hollywood Hills Clinic and initiatives with the Bright Hope

Clinic. Flo glanced over and could see a petite woman with mahogany hair and hazel eyes smiling and nodding at everything that Freya was saying, and Flo recognized her as Mila Brightman, who ran the Bright Hope Clinic, but it was the look that James was shooting at Mila that caught Flo's attention immediately. There was underlying tension there, something Flo recognized as akin to her own feelings regarding Nate and their shared passionate kiss.

Flo couldn't help but wonder if there was something going on between James and Mila. James was usually so reserved in press conferences, so detached and cool, but this was different. Something was bubbling just under the surface of James Rothsberg.

Just like something was threatening to bubble out from her.

You can do this. Just stay focused.

All she had to do was keep reminding herself that as soon as Nate found out about her health condition, about how she had almost died from chronic kidney failure as a child because of complications from her premature birth and spending a month in a NICU, he'd turn tail and run. Like all of them did.

"And as part of the Bright Hope Clinic's collaboration with The Hollywood Hills Clinic, we're pleased to announce that our dream team of Dr. Florence Chiu and Dr. Nathaniel King, two of the best transplant surgeons in the country, will be taking on Eva Martinez's case while they continue to provide care to Kyle Francis." Freya motioned for Flo to get up and approach the microphone.

You can do this.

There was a round of applause and as soon as she got to the microphone she was hammered by a loud din of questions being asked rapid-fire. James stood up and bent over the microphone.

"Please, one question at a time. I'm sure Dr. Chiu would be more than happy to answer all your questions." His tone was such that his word wouldn't be challenged. The din quieted down and he stepped away, leaving Flo up there by herself.

"You, sir. What's your question?" Flo pointed to a balding, pudgy man in the front row.

"Photographs of you and Dr. King have arisen that gives rise to questions about the state of security at The Hollywood Hills Clinic. Patients are wondering if their privacy will be protected and whether their doctors' focus will be on them, or will it be solely on who to hop into bed with next?"

Flo could feel her cheeks burning with a flame of embarrassment. "I can assure you that *my* focus is solely on my patients' care."

Nate stood up. "Dr. Chiu and I are in a committed relationship. We went on the rooftop after a successful surgery involving Mr. Francis and got carried away. Are you telling me that you've never got carried away celebrating with your significant other before?"

Nate then flashed a dazzling smile to the audience, which had them all laughing.

Oh, he was good.

"That still doesn't address the privacy and security concerns," the balding reporter called.

"The picture was snapped by a paparazzo from an office window across from the clinic. We can't control what happens outside our perimeters, but he was not able to get any photographs inside our facility, neither was he able to take photographs of our patients," Freya said.

"What about the paramedic that leaked the information?" another reporter asked.

"My understanding is he's been reprimanded and he will not be allowed back on The Hollywood Hills Clinic property in a capacity where he'll have access to confidential health information," James said brusquely.

Once they were satisfied another reporter stepped forward. "How long have you and Dr. King been in a relationship?"

"For a couple of months. We met to discuss Mr. Francis's care while our patient was in California to shoot a movie."

Nate nodded and touched the small of her back. Just the simple touch made goose pimples break out on her skin. Good thing he couldn't feel them.

"Can you tell us a little bit about Mr. Francis's procedure?"

"Of course. Mr. Francis is in congestive heart failure, but because he's been in heart failure for some time, this has put a strain on his already weak lungs. Mr. Francis had a pre-existing struggle with asthma for many years. Because his lungs are so damaged by the extra strain his heart is causing, he will require a heart and lung transplant. We were hoping to perform a domino procedure, but now that Mr. Francis is on a left ventricular assist device, he is no longer a candidate. We will have to wait for a set of lungs and a heart that matches Mr. Francis's blood type, but the LVAD will prolong his life while he waits."

Nate gave her a thumbs-up and Flo gave an inward sigh of relief. She sat back down next to Nate and he took her hand and held it. It was reassuring and made her feel good, but then she remembered this was all an act.

He'd pretty much said that he wasn't interested in her and that their kiss had been a mistake.

That's what you wanted, wasn't it?

"Now, if there are no more questions we'll conclude this press conference," Freya said. "Please make sure you take the statement with you. If you have any other questions, please don't hesitate to contact me. Thank you all for coming."

Flo took another deep breath.

"See, that wasn't too bad," Nate said, but he didn't let go of her hand as the journalists filtered out of the room slowly.

"No. It wasn't." She let go of his hand and got up to leave, but Freya and James were talking to the side and motioned for her over.

Oh, no. Now what?

"Good job, Flo," Freya said.

James nodded. "Yes. You handled that well."

"Thank you."

"I think that will help salvage the reputation of The Hollywood Hills Clinic and help reinforce our joint effort with the Bright Hope Clinic."

"I think it will," Mila said, joining them and extending a hand to take Flo's. "Dr. Mila Brightman. A pleasure to meet you, Dr. Chiu. I'm so pleased that you and Dr. King will be working on Eva Martinez's case."

"It will be a pleasure to do so," Flo responded.

"All this good publicity for the clinic will put my mind at ease," said Freya.

"A good thing, given your condition—" James cut off abruptly at the sharp stare from his sister and the surprised looks from the rest of the group.

"Well, since *some* people clearly don't know how to keep a secret, I guess the cat's out of the bag—I'm pregnant!" Freya announced.

James smiled sheepishly. "I'm so happy for you, Freya."

Then he turned to Mila and Flo noticed something pass between them. It was as if he wanted to embrace Dr. Brightman but held himself back. She couldn't help but wonder what was going on there, but, then, she liked her privacy, as well. She felt a bit humiliated that that private mistake of a kiss between her and Nate had been caught on camera so it wasn't her place to pry.

"Well, I'll leave you all to it," Flo said. "I'm going to go check on my new patient. I assume that Eva Martinez has been admitted to the transplant floor?"

Freya nodded. "Yes, thank you, Flo."

Flo walked away briskly. She was done with awkward situations. It was bad enough she had to be pretend to be in a relationship with Nate. That was uncomfortable, especially with the way he affected her.

She needed to focus on her new patient.

Eva's case struck close to home for her. Only, for Flo, it hadn't been her mother who had donated a kidney to her. Flo's kidney donation had come from a deceased organ donor. Being of mixed heritage had caused a bit of a cross-match problem for Flo. It didn't happen often, but Flo's case had been a hard one from the moment she'd been born prematurely thirty years ago.

If it hadn't been for that anonymous donor, who, of course, had sadly lost their life, Flo would've lost hers. Of course her *năinai* had always said she'd been a tough cookie from the moment she'd been born. Flo had been fighting her whole life. It's why she fought so hard for others; it's why she wanted to live in the moment.

Even though pretending to be Nate's girlfriend made her feel uncomfortable, because it was a temptation that she was in danger of indulging in, she was going to do what had been asked of her. What could it hurt?

It could hurt your heart.

Flo shook that thought away. This wasn't a serious re-lationship. It would *never* be a serious relationship. She didn't have serious relationships because of her health is-sues and she'd made her peace with that a long time ago.

Have you?

She caught sight of Nate in the hallway, talking with a group of doctors and what looked like members of Kyle's management team. Just the sight of Nate standing there made her heart flutter with insatiable need. She turned on her heel and quickly headed in the opposite direction.

Focus, Flo. She had to forget the carnal urges that Nate stirred in her. She had to remind herself that this was all an act. This would be fun. She could do this. What did she have to lose?

Pretending to be his was going to be so difficult. So dangerous. Even if she was a tough cookie, like her *năinai* said.

Nate glanced over his shoulder to see Flo retreating in the other direction, which was unlike her. She had never seemed fazed or frightened by anything before. She hadn't backed down from him when they'd first met.

He admired that about her.

Don't think about her that way.

He tried to turn his attention back the conversation he'd been having, not that he could really remember what he'd been talking about. It hadn't really been that im-portant because all of his focus had been on Flo, and it bothered him that he was so absorbed with her that he'd agreed to play along with The Hills' ridiculous request.

His hospital in New York would never have asked him to do such a thing, but then again the hospital in New York wasn't a private upscale clinic that prided it-self on the security of its clients. Neither did he like the fact that Freya had conspired with Kyle's management team about the idea.

Only problem was, he wasn't a good actor.

A few years ago and he might've gone along with it, but now he liked to maintain control in all aspects of his life. One little slip and that reckless man he'd once been started to creep toward the surface.

And he couldn't let that happen. Only when he was around Flo, she made him forget his control. He lost all reason. That's why he'd pulled her into that kiss on the roof and got them into trouble in the first place.

They were in this mess because of him.

"Dr. King?"

Nate turned and saw James Rothsberg standing behind him. Beside James was an attractive redhead.

"Are we interrupting?" James asked sardonically.

"No. Not at all."

James nodded. "This is Dr. Mila Brightman from the Bright Hope Clinic. She wanted to meet you."

Mila stuck out her hand. "It's a pleasure to meet you, Dr. King."

"The pleasure is all mine."

It was then that Nate caught a flash of something in James's eyes, something akin to jealousy or a silent warning maybe to keep his distance, and Nate couldn't help but wonder if there was or had been something between Mila Brightman and James Rothsberg.

Not that it was Nate's concern, but he couldn't miss that underlying tension between them, the same current that ran between him and Flo.

It's all in your head. You're paranoid.

"I want to thank you and Dr. Chiu for working on Eva. She's a special child," Mila said.

"It's no trouble. I'm here and glad to help. If you'll

excuse me, I'm going to check on my patient." Nate extracted himself from that situation. The tension was uncomfortable and when he glanced back briefly he could see the awkwardness between James and Mila. They barely said anything, barely looked at each other before wandering off on their own separate ways.

This was exactly the reason why he didn't want to get involved with anyone. Especially not at work. His focus was surgery.

He should just tell Freya that he wasn't going to play along with this PR stunt, but where would that leave Flo?

Who cares?

Only he did. Just a bit, because it was his fault, his weakness that had got them into this situation. If he had been stronger he wouldn't have been tempted by Flo. He could've kept his distance. He should've kept his distance. He could do this.

Who are you kidding?

He had to get out of the hospital, had to head to his hotel and swim. He had to relieve this tension that was building up inside him, because if he didn't he was liable to crack and do something he would enjoy thoroughly but also deeply regret.

CHAPTER FIVE

WHAT AM I DOING? What am I doing?

The scent of chlorine stung her nose. She'd never really liked the smell of chlorine, probably because it reminded her of the many hours she'd spent poolside, watching her brother and sister swim competitively, something she'd never been able to do because she'd been sick for so long.

Thinking about her siblings swimming made her think about how she'd always wanted to learn how to dive. It was on her bucket list, but she'd never found the time.

And standing poolside at Nate King's hotel, watching said hottie swim countless laps, was not the time to start. She was having a hard time not staring at him, the way he moved through the water.

She'd wanted to talk to him before he'd left the hospital. If they were going to participate in this facade then she was going to get her facts straight. She was nothing if not efficient.

That's why she kept lists. She was organized, and when she did something, she did it right. If she was going to be Dr. Nate King's pretend girlfriend, she was going to do it right.

Except cleaning. She was a bit scatterbrained when it came to cleaning her apartment.

At least her office and workspace were organized.

He finished swimming and pulled himself out of the water at the far end of the pool. Flo tried not to stare at his muscular thighs and tight butt only covered in wet spandex. When he'd wrapped a white cotton towel around his waist, partially obscuring his six pack, only then did she hold her head high and walk toward him.

"Nate," she said.

He spun around in surprise, raking a hand through his dripping-wet beach-blond locks.

"Dr. Chiu."

"It's Flo, remember. We are dating after all." She laughed nervously, but he didn't smile. "I was hoping to talk to you before you left the clinic tonight but I just missed you. So that's why I'm here."

"About what?" he asked, picking up a second towel and drying off his face.

"About our 'relationship'." She used air quotes to emphasize it.

He groaned. "Now?"

"Are you busy? Do you have a prior engagement?" she asked, crossing her arms.

Nate dropped the towel he was wiping his face with and smiled, but that smile wasn't the cheeky one he usually gave her. It was a bit predatory and made her nervous.

"Would you be jealous if I did?" He took a step closer. "If I did, what would you do?"

"No. I'm not jealous, but for the sake of the clinic and our patients it would be bad form to have plans."

He chuckled and then snorted sardonically. "Would it? Don't you think this whole charade is bad form?"

Yes. Only she didn't say that out loud because she didn't understand PR like Freya and Mila did. Both of them thought this charade would be a good idea.

"We're just smoothing over a tricky situation," Flo said.

He arched his eyebrows. "Is that a fact? And have you canceled all your private engagements? Dumped your boyfriends?"

She sighed impatiently. "What is your obsession with my boyfriends?"

"Well, I don't think it would be good form for our charade if you had a couple of boyfriends lingering about."

"As I told you before, I don't have a boyfriend. As for private engagements, surgery is my life."

He grunted again and pushed past her. "How did you know where to find me?"

"Freya told me." She followed him out of the pool toward a bank of elevators.

"Of course she did." He shook his head.

"Well, shouldn't I know where my 'boyfriend' lives? Especially since we've been together for some time?"

"Good point. I never really thought about that. Deception really isn't my forte." The elevator doors opened and he stepped in. "Aren't you coming up?"

"To your room?" She hoped her voice didn't squeak too much because the idea of going up to his room was not on her agenda tonight. She couldn't go up to his room.

That was not part of the plan.

He grinned at her. That predatory grin again. "Yes. Play along, right? Isn't that what you told me?"

"How about I wait for you down here? We can have a drink in the hotel lobby."

"Now, how would that look to the paparazzi milling about at the concierge's desk?"

Flo glance over her shoulder and saw the press.

Hell.

She jumped into the elevator, the door closing just as

a photographer caught sight of them. That would've been bad and their cover would've been blown.

Nate was laughing at her. "Smooth move, Dr. Chiu."

"When did you notice him?"

"A while ago."

"You could've warned me."

"I did. That's why you're in the elevator now instead of waiting for me in the hotel's bar."

"I'd prefer to wait in the lobby bar," she mumbled.

"Why?" he asked.

Because it's safer.

"I don't know you. I don't think it's appropriate to go up to your hotel room."

Nate laughed. The elevator dinged and they stepped off. She followed him down the hall to the end. He swiped the key card and opened the door. Flo followed him inside, just on the off chance the paparazzi followed them up here. She shut the door and was surprised by the large suite. It was like a small apartment. There was a bedroom that Nate had disappeared into, a living room and small kitchenette.

She set her purse down on the counter and wandered to the huge windows, where the Los Angeles skyline lit up the night. It was a gorgeous night. Clear, but it wasn't like you could see the sky, not with all the light pollution from LA. Nate's suite had a large balcony and a hot tub tucked away in the corner.

"There are drinks in the fridge. I'm going to have a quick shower," Nate said from around the door of his bedroom.

"Okay, thanks."

Nate nodded and shut the door to his bedroom. It wasn't too long before Flo heard the shower on through the closed door and she tried not to think about the fact that Nate was naked and in it.

This was a bad idea.

She could've just waited until he came to work the next day and talked to him there, but no. She'd got it in her head that this would be a better idea and now she couldn't remember for the life of her why she'd thought that.

Probably because she hadn't expected to find him half-naked, swimming in a pool, and then be forced to come up to his opulent suite and wait while he showered in the next room. This was an experience that was *not* on her bucket list.

Flo took a seat on the edge of the couch and just waited. She tried to keep her mind occupied on something else. Anything to take her mind off what was going on in the next room and how he'd looked just wrapped in a towel, fresh from a swim. The only men she'd seen built like that were either in the movies or magazines. She'd never seen one up close and personal.

She'd worked on Hollywood's rich and famous at The Hollywood Hills Clinic, but what was on screen versus reality had opened to her eyes to the whole magical mystery of Hollywood's elite. Photo editing was a beautiful thing indeed.

She often wished she could edit herself in real life. Maybe then she could erase the large scar on her abdomen and that way no one would ever need to know that she'd had a kidney transplant. That she'd been sick.

If Johnny hadn't known, he wouldn't have treated her differently.

Maybe they'd still be together. Then she wouldn't have kissed Nate and be in this situation, faking a relationship and being in his hotel room with him naked in the shower. In the next room. Of course, that's not how it had happened at all, because that's not how real life worked. There had been no photo-editing solution and her disease had frightened Johnny away.

He'd made it clear he didn't want to get involved with her, not when there was a possibility that at any time in the near future that donor organ could fail and she might die. No one wanted to get involved with a woman who didn't have the greatest odds of staying alive.

Kidney survival rates were good, but they weren't perfect.

Kidneys could fail.

Especially when you'd had a chronic kidney disease as a child and had suffered kidney failure at fourteen. Following dialysis for a year and a near-death experience, she'd received her new lease on life.

And since that time she'd tried to live her life to the fullest.

Getting married and having a family had always been on her bucket list, until she'd learned the true nature of most men. When Johnny had run scared and left her heartbroken, she'd scratched that secret hope off her list.

A husband, romance and love were not meant to be. She'd made her peace with that, but now, because of a foolish and irrational moment on top of The Hollywood Hills Clinic, she found herself thrust into a situation she'd long given up on.

It's fake, though. It's not real.

Still, the idea made her uncomfortable because she was going to have to be really careful to keep her feelings out of it. She could have fun, but she couldn't let Nate get too close, because once Kyle Francis was on the mend, Dr. Nathaniel King would be returning to New York and she would be alone again.

"Did you want something to drink?"

Flo startled to see a freshly showered and dressed Nate standing in the doorway. He was dressed very much the same as he'd been when she'd first laid eyes on him. When he'd come out of that helicopter looking sexy as hell.

Don't think about it.

"How about we go downstairs?" Flo asked, tearing her gaze away from Nate.

"Well, first I think we should go over some ground rules for this whole charade, and I don't think that those ground rules should be discussed downstairs with paparazzi milling about. They were told we've been going out for some time. You can't be all skittish and embarrassed around me."

"I'm not skittish or embarrassed. I'm professional."

Nate rolled his eyes and shook his head. "You can't be professional with your boyfriend."

"Boyfriend sounds like we're in junior high or something."

"Lover, then?"

Warmth flooded her cheeks and her whole body quivered with the quick burn of arousal as an image of Nate, naked and pressed against her, filled her mind.

Lover.

That was something she was not intimately familiar with, but she wished she was.

She cleared her throat. "Fine. I can be relaxed around you."

Nate grinned, leaning over the polished marble counter in his kitchenette. "Can you?"

"Of course I can."

"Prove it."

"How?" she asked.

"Kiss me again."

* * *

Nate had no idea what had come over him when he'd asked Flo to kiss him. It had just seemed the natural thing to do and he'd be an idiot if he said he didn't want to kiss her again. Who wouldn't want to kiss her again? And he knew by the flush creeping up her long slender neck to her cheeks that she was feeling it, too.

She wanted him, but was holding back.

Like you should be, too.

And that was when it struck him that he'd done something he really shouldn't have, and that no woman since Serena had affected him this way.

He'd been attracted to other women, but he'd always managed to keep them at a distance. Then he'd met Flo. He tried to tell himself over and over again that the kiss on the rooftop had only been his relief at having been able to stabilize Kyle. They'd been able to extend Kyle's life while he waited for his new heart and lungs. That relief had caused him to let his guard down, so what was this?

This wasn't relief.

Even though he really didn't want to play in this charade that Freya Rothsberg had cooked up, he really had no choice, that's why he threw up his walls again. He was determined that even though on the outside, for all intents and purposes, he was Flo's significant other, he wasn't going to let her in.

He wasn't going to let his guard down around her.

At least, that's what he was going to do in theory. Twenty minutes with her and she was in his hotel suite, sitting on his couch only five feet away from him, looking as sinfully sexy as ever. Her long black hair, which she usually wore up, was loose over her shoulders. There was a bit of make-up on her, not much, but the red lipstick on her lips just accentuated the fullness of them. Add the blush to those high, round cheeks and he was a lost man.

He forgot that Flo was off-limits to him, just like every woman had been since Serena. Yet here he was, asking Flo to kiss him again. And he wanted to kiss her. So badly.

"Pardon?" she said, breaking the silence.

"I think you heard me."

"I don't think that's a wise idea, Nate. Do you?"

It's not.

"Why? You want to show the world that we're together. We have to be at ease with each other so we can be believable."

What are you doing?

"Believable, but also professional. So I don't think kissing you is the wisest idea." She tossed her hair over her shoulder. "You certainly like to goad me, don't you?"

Nate's eyes twinkled. "Perhaps, but it's so easy."

She glared at him and then smiled. "I'm highly competitive and I don't like to have my buttons pushed."

"I gathered that, or it wouldn't be so easy to push them."

Flo nodded. "Perhaps we can go downstairs and get that drink? Discuss Eva's case and our plan of attack?"

"Okay, but still I think you should kiss me."

She grinned in a willful way that spelled trouble for him. "I do like to hear you beg."

He rolled his eyes as she walked past him toward the door. On one hand he was extremely relieved that she hadn't kissed him, but he knew that if he kissed her again he would lose himself completely and carry her off to his bed, which wasn't far away.

And taking her to bed would be good, so deliciously good, but only for a short time. He didn't want to hurt her, not when they had possibly months of working together while they waited for Kyle's heart and lung transplant.

That would be awkward and horrible for everyone.

It was better this way.

That's what he had to keep telling himself to get over the smidgen of disappointment he had that she hadn't taken him up on his offer and kissed him.

Instead, as they walked down the hall toward the elevator, he reached down and took her hand in his. That small delicate hand that he'd admired so much during Kyle's LVAD surgery.

"What're you doing?" she asked, surprised.

"The paparazzi could be still downstairs. This way, there won't be any questions."

"Oh…right. Good point."

Nate could tell that she was nervous, and he liked that he had that effect on her. Serena had been the same when they'd first dated, but not for long. Maybe one date, because one date was all it had taken and they'd been in bed together and then heading off on a crazy adventure.

Don't think about Serena.

If he thought about Serena he'd pull away from Flo again and then the press would pick up on the fact that this was all just a charade. He had to remember what it was like to just let things happen and not control every aspect of his life, which was a hard thing for him to do because control allowed him to focus on saving lives.

There was no room in his heart for love or romance. Not again.

"You okay?" Flo asked as they rode down to the lobby in the elevator.

"Yeah, why?"

"I don't know. You just tensed up."

"I'm fine." He tried to give her a reassuring smile.

"I'm really fine, it's just that I don't like this. I don't like deception."

"I know. Neither do I, but it's for the clinic."

"Right. The clinic." The doors dinged and opened and they stepped out into the lobby. He knew that press guy was lingering around somewhere. It felt like there were a million eyes on them as they walked hand in hand toward the hotel's bar. Even when they found a private booth far in the corner of the bar, he still felt like they were under a microscope, and it made him uneasy.

It was only after the waiter had brought them their drinks that Flo said, "I feel like we're being watched."

"We are." He took a sip of his coffee. "Is this your first time working on someone as famous as Kyle Francis?"

"No. I've worked on some others, it's just The Hollywood Hills Clinic's security has never been breached before."

"Sorry about that."

Flo shrugged and took a sip of her water. "It's unfortunate but there's nothing we can do."

Nate chuckled. "Look at us, we've come to a bar and we don't even order alcoholic drinks."

"I don't drink," Flo said, and then she blushed, clearing her throat. "I mean, I have to get up early tomorrow and I don't want to drink tonight."

"Rounds?"

She nodded. "I want to check on Kyle and Eva, our two VIP patients."

"I'm not on rounds. I have privileges, but no regular patients beyond Kyle and Eva."

"You could always round with me." She smiled at him. It was warm, inviting and friendly, and now he could clearly remember why he'd kissed her on the rooftop. He wanted a piece of that. He wanted to feel that warmth.

"Sure. Thanks."

"No problem." She set her water glass down and glanced at the watch on her arm. "Oh, my, is that the time? It's almost ten."

"Ten isn't late."

"It is when you're rounding at five in the morning." Flo sighed. "I have to go."

"I'll walk you out." Nate signed the bill to his suite, the whole couple of bucks for the coffee, and walked her out of the bar to the hotel entrance. "Did you drive yourself?"

"I don't drive. I live close to the clinic. I usually just ride my bike."

"You don't drive?"

"I never learned, but it's on my bucket list." Then she blushed again.

"Bucket list? Usually that's for people who don't have a lot of time left. Unless I'm mistaken, Dr. Chiu, you have many years left."

"Oh, yeah, of course. It's nothing really. Just stuff I want to do before I… Anyway, I'd better go. The doorman can flag down a taxi for me."

"Sure. I'll see you tomorrow." Nate walked her outside and they stood there while the doorman waved down a taxi. When the taxi pulled up Flo turned quickly and pressed a sweet, light kiss against his lips. It caught him off guard and his blood heated. He fought back the urge to take her in his arms and deepen the kiss, make it last.

Which was a dangerous thing indeed.

"See you tomorrow," she said, not looking at him as she climbed into the cab.

As the cab drove away he stood there, his blood burning through his veins at just the simple butterfly kiss that had been brushed against his lips. So innocent, so sweet. It left him wanting more.

So much more.

CHAPTER SIX

FLO DOWNED HER second cup of coffee, which had two shots of espresso in it. She didn't know what had made her reach out and kiss Nate, because she'd had no plans to do that. Especially not after he'd basically dared her to kiss him in his hotel suite.

When he'd asked her that, it had taken all her willpower not to leap into his arms and kiss him again. To experience that heat and heady sensation he'd stirred within her since he'd first kissed her on the rooftop. Nate was incredibly sexy and Flo had never been attracted to a man so strongly before. So much so that she almost forgot herself and the fact that she'd sworn off all romantic entanglements.

Besides, Nate would run as soon as he realized what was going on with her. She tried to tell herself that maybe he would understand as he was a transplant surgeon himself, but then maybe that would make him back off all the more, because he would understand better than anyone what her body had been through.

Still, she'd been a fool and kissed him while waiting for the taxi, even though it had been for the press. She was pretty sure there would be pictures of them kissing and that would make Freya happy.

There was a lot of press camped outside The Hollywood Hills Clinic. She could see them lurking in shadows, waiting for something, anything, to give them juicy details about Kyle Francis and his surgeons who were in love.

Flo snorted. *Love. Sure.*

She didn't believe in love. Well, not for her anyway. Once she'd believed in love, but then love had turned on her. There was love. She'd seen it in her parents. They'd overcome a lot of odds and barriers in their way to be together. They came from different worlds yet that hadn't mattered to them in the end.

For them it worked.

Love couldn't work for her. Not when she couldn't promise any length of time to anyone. It wasn't really fair to someone else.

Flo groaned and crushed the empty coffee cup, tossing it in the garbage. Last week none of this had been an issue. Last week she'd been free of Dr. Nathaniel King. Last week she'd just been a great surgeon, with a stupid bucket list and a job that hadn't let her think about her personal life.

Last week she'd been happy. Now she was miserable.

Are you so sure about that?

"Flo!"

Flo turned to see Freya walking toward her. "Freya, I'm surprised to see you here so early."

"I couldn't sleep and had morning sickness." Freya held out a paper. "I'm glad to see that you and Dr. King are keeping up appearances."

Flo glanced down at the tabloid paper and saw photos of her kiss with Nate. That quick, impulsive kiss that had burned its memory on her lips and taunted her all night, which was the reason why she'd downed two large black coffees with espresso shots, because she hadn't been able to stop thinking about it all night.

And now seeing it plastered over the tabloids reminded her of how hot that moment had been, and how foolish. She was willing to climb a mountain or do some other high-adrenaline sport, but when it came to the possibility of romance, she wasn't willing to let her heart get involved.

It was too dangerous.

"Ah," Flo said nervously. "Yeah, well, I thought I would pay Dr. King a visit to talk about our arrangement."

"Well, keep up the good work. Tomorrow night there's a dinner with some possible investors and they want the dream team to attend. It's business casual and will be at Dan Tana's at eight-thirty."

"Dinner? I...I have a shift tomorrow. Rounds in the evening."

"I have another doctor covering for you, one of your fellows." Freya glanced over her shoulder and waved. "Dr. King, can you come here a moment, please?"

Flo froze and was very aware the moment that Nate walked up behind her. She could smell the clean spicy scent of his body wash. She'd been very aware of it when she'd impulsively kissed him.

"Good morning, ladies." He had already changed into scrubs and had a white lab coat with an identification card. The white of the lab coat accentuated his tan and the blueness of his eyes.

"I was just telling Flo how pleased I was to see you two cooperating." Freya handed Nate the tabloid. Flo watched his expression carefully, but if it affected him she had no clue. He just nodded, smiled charmingly and handed the paper back to Freya.

"Just doing our part," he said.

"I was just telling Flo that there's a dinner tomorrow night at Dan Tana's. Business casual as we'll be meeting with investors." Freya tucked the paper under her arm. "I have to run. I look forward to seeing you both tomorrow."

Flo didn't even have a chance to say no, she didn't want to have dinner with a bunch of investors and pretend to be Nate's girlfriend, but she really had no choice.

Her job was on the line.

If she didn't play her part then people would stop coming to The Hollywood Hills Clinic, investors would stop giving money and the clinic could shut down. Then she couldn't help Eva, and she was very on board with this partnership with the Bright Hope Clinic and providing pro bono surgery to kids like Eva.

To kids who reminded her of herself.

"Dan Tana's is a nice place," Nate remarked. "I used to go there a lot as a kid."

"I thought you were from New York?" Flo said.

"I work in New York, but I'm a native Californian."

Flo snorted. "That doesn't surprise me. You have the look of a beach boy."

Nate fell into step beside her. "Where are you from?"

"Seattle," Flo responded, offhand. "Though my father is from Beijing and my mother is from the Deep South. They felt Seattle was a nice halfway point to raise their family."

Flo smiled as she thought of her family. She hadn't talked to them in a while as she'd been so busy. Actually, she was surprised that her father wasn't calling her cell phone every two minutes to question what was going on and why she was kissing men on rooftops.

Her parents had always been a little overprotective, trying to keep her wrapped up in cotton wool, like she was some kind of fragile piece of crystal that was about to shatter into a million pieces.

Which was why when she'd got her kidney she'd rebelled a bit. Pushed the boundaries and decided to study medicine at Johns Hopkins across the country, almost a world away from her parents. After spending most of her childhood basically in a bubble, her first taste of freedom had been an amazing rush.

It's why she had the bucket list.

So many things she wanted to do. So little time.

"So you mentioned learning to drive is on this bucket list," Nate said casually.

"It is. I just don't have time to take lessons. My work here takes a lot of my time."

"I can teach you."

Flo laughed. "Yeah, right."

"Who better to teach you? I've driven in two of the busiest cities in America—Los Angeles and New York City."

"You have a point, but when? I don't have time."

"How about tonight?"

Flo cocked an eyebrow. "Tonight? You're going to teach me to drive tonight?"

"Sure. I can't take you out on the streets, but I know a place out of the city where there's an abandoned parking lot and plenty of room for you to make mistakes."

"Okay. I get off at three."

"I know." Nate took a step back away from her. "I have to make a phone call to my office in New York. I'll meet you up at Eva's room in twenty."

"Sure, leave all the grunt work to me," she teased.

He just smiled at her and disappeared down a hall, leaving her standing there absolutely perplexed about what had just happened. She told herself she was going to be stronger. When she had to make public appearances with him, she was going to play the part of the girlfriend, but this learning-to-drive date she'd just made with him, that was just them. That wasn't something public.

It was just going be the two of them.

And that thought made her nervous.

Don't think about it.

She put her hands under the sanitary gel dispenser. Right now she couldn't think about that. Right now she had to be a surgeon. She glanced through the window to see Eva, so sick and in bed with an IV and looking so lost. Her mother was next to her, holding her hand.

It tore at Flo's heart. She'd been there.

She'd felt that way and her parents had been there. Only her mother hadn't been the one to give her a kidney, so she couldn't even begin to fathom the kind of strain that Ms. Martinez was going through or the amount of time it would take for both of them to recover, both emotionally, physically and financially.

Right now, this was Flo's focus. This was her passion, saving lives, especially giving a chance to a little girl who reminded her so much of herself that it was almost haunting.

"Good morning, Ms. Martinez and Eva. I'm Dr. Flo Chiu and I'll be one of the surgeons on your case."

The phone call back to New York had taken longer than expected, but by the end of the call he had been assured that all his patients were being taken good care of and that his practice was in safe hands. For so long Kyle had been his main focus, he didn't really have a lot of other patients who needed him as much.

Kyle had been very specific that Nate's sole focus was to be on him, and he paid him well enough that he didn't have to take on too many patients, which meant he wasn't really missed in New York.

Nate didn't have friends in New York City. Colleagues, yes, but not any people he would consider friends. Neither did he have any family in New York. His parents were here in California and he definitely didn't have a significant other.

No one missed him and he didn't mind much.

He might've been chomping at the bit to get back to his practice, but being around Flo and working with her was exciting. It was fun, and that kiss she'd given him had kept him up all night.

So to take his mind off it he'd spent the night going over Eva's case. It had been a year since he'd done a kidney transplant with a live donor. Kyle had been his focus and any other cases he took on were usually complicated. Nate hadn't realized that for a long time he'd been focusing solely on the heart and lung. He'd had to brush up on his reading about kidney transplants. What concerned him most was that Ms. Martinez was a single parent. The sole breadwinner. Donating a kidney would put her out of commission for a long time. Weeks, for sure. Even if they did the retrieval laparoscopically and reduced her recovery time, she'd still be off for a couple of weeks.

Ms. Martinez was a waitress. She would need a month to heal from a laparoscopic procedure. She wouldn't be able to lift heavy objects and would still tire easily.

Even then, Nate wasn't sure that Ms. Martinez was a candidate for a laparoscopic procedure. He would have to do some more tests to be sure. Get some better MRI images.

Ms. Martinez could become destitute while she recovered. Being a waitress was a minimum-wage job, one that probably didn't have medical leave coverage.

Eva was pretty stable, so maybe in the family's best interests they should wait for a deceased donor.

When he got to Eva's room he paused in the hallway. He saw Flo sitting on the end of Eva's bed and she was playing cards with her. Nate smiled. When he'd first met Flo he'd thought she would be a bit uptight, reserved, but seeing her with Eva and playing a game of cards, well, he couldn't help but smile.

She was so warm with Eva.

There were so many layers to Flo; she was so intriguing. At times she was so prudish and then the next moment she was giving him a kiss that made him want her more than anything. Other times she was standoffish, but then could give a good quip that got through his thick-walled exterior. Back in New York City he had a reputation of being hardheaded. Someone you didn't want to mess with.

The moment he'd tried that with her, Flo had been right in his face and giving back as good as he could give her, but there was something Flo was hiding. She'd mentioned a bucket list and had then brushed it off as something silly. Only Nate knew there was something more there, and he shouldn't care what it was because he didn't want to get too close to her. He couldn't get too close to her, but he did care.

He wanted to know all of her, even though nothing could come of it. This relationship wasn't a relationship. It was just a facade. And when Kyle was on the mend and this pro bono case was done, he would pack his bags and head back to New York and his life.

Just like she would go back to hers, because this wasn't real. It was all fake.

And that thought made him sad, because just for one

moment he was wishing it wasn't all fake, that Flo and him were really dating.

Don't think like that.

He shook that thought from his head, disgusted with himself for allowing himself to think like that again. For letting his mind head down that path again. He was here to do work; he was here to save two lives.

This whole situation was temporary. There wouldn't be any permanence. There couldn't be any permanence to it.

He knocked on the door and plastered his best smile on his face. One he knew well and had practiced. A shield to the armor he wore every day to keep people out. "Am I interrupting?"

"Yes," Flo said, smiling and winking at Eva, who giggled. "Eva, this is your other surgeon. This is Dr. Nathaniel King."

Nate stood beside Flo and Eva smiled up at Nate.

"It's nice to meet you, Eva," Nate said.

"Nice to meet you, too, Dr. King." For a twelve-year-old girl she had excellent manners.

"You can call me Nate. I've just come to check your vitals. Is that okay?"

Eva's brow furrowed and she looked at Flo with concern. "Will it hurt?"

"No, this is just a vital check. No needles." Flo set down her cards and got off the bed, moving the swinging table out of the way. "Nate is super nice."

"I promise you it won't hurt at all." Nate pulled out his stethoscope. "I just want to have a listen to your heart first. Is that okay?"

"Sure." Eva sat up the best she could and Nate listened to her chest.

"Deep breaths for me, Eva." He moved his stethoscope and listened. "One more for me."

"Is that it?" Eva asked.

"Just blood pressure now."

Eva winced. "I don't like the squeeze."

"It's just for a second. It's nothing. Trust me, I would know," Flo said reassuringly, squeezing Eva's foot under the blanket. "You need to relax. Nate will get a better reading if you relax."

Eva nodded and Nate put the cuff on her and took her blood pressure. It was as good as it could be for a young girl in renal failure.

"Thank you, Eva. Do you mind if I borrow Flo for a moment?"

"Sure." Eva leaned back and picked up her cards.

"No cheating!" Flo warned, giving her a wink that caused Eva to laugh.

They stepped out of the room and Nate shut the door. Flo frowned and crossed her arms. "Is there something wrong? I checked her when I first arrived and her vitals were fine."

"Her vitals are fine. I was just hoping that Ms. Martinez would be around so that I could talk to her about her side of the donation."

"Ms. Martinez had to make some arrangements. She's going to be out of commission for some time, as well."

"That's what I wanted to talk to her about. Eva is stable, so why don't we wait for a deceased donor?"

Flo's brow furrowed further. "Ms. Martinez is a match. Her cross-match is the best I've seen in a long time. Why would we wait? Waiting just puts Eva in danger."

"Ms. Martinez is a single mother. She could continue working while Eva recovered here."

Flo shook her head. "The cross-match is almost perfect. A cross-match from a deceased donor wouldn't be as good. Ms. Martinez won't wait while her child sits on a list, she's done that. It's in their file. That's why she went to the Bright Hope Clinic, because she is the perfect donor for Eva. Eva is less likely to reject her mother's kidney."

"Less likely, though, Dr. Chiu. There's still a chance. There's always a high chance of rejection."

Flo's spine stiffened, her face unreadable. It was as if he'd slapped her across the face. "I'm *very* well aware of that, Dr. King. You don't have to remind me of that. I'm still head surgeon on this case. Ms. Martinez knows the risks. She doesn't want to wait, she doesn't want her daughter to get worse. It's her gift to give Eva. We're not going to discuss this matter further or try to convince her of anything different."

"I would feel better if I talked to Ms. Martinez all the same."

Flo glared at him. "Fine, but let it be on your head. I doubt you'll convince her. She wants to save her child and what she's doing is an amazing thing."

She tried to turn and storm off, but he grabbed her by her elbow. "What has got into you?"

"Nothing, I'm just annoyed that you're trying to talk a woman, who knows all the facts because her daughter has been fighting renal failure her whole life, out of saving her daughter's life."

Nate sighed. "I'm not trying to talk her out of it. I just don't want to see her lose her job."

"She won't," Flo said, calming down. "Her work is being compliant. Mila Brightman talked to them about the situation."

Nate nodded. "Okay. That's great. I'm glad she knows everything. I wasn't trying to endanger the patient. Please trust me, because if you don't trust me here, you won't trust me in the OR and I need you to trust me in the OR when we work on Eva and Kyle."

Mollified, Flo nodded. "I trust you, Nate. I trust you as a surgeon. It's just…this is a touchy subject for me."

Intrigued, Nate let go of his grip on her. "Why?"

"I knew someone who suffered a long time, waiting for a deceased donor who was a good cross-match. A young girl, like Eva, whose parents would've given their kidneys, but they weren't a match."

Nate nodded. "I understand."

"Do you?"

"Yes," Nate said wearily. "I lost someone I cared for. Someone who was waiting on organs."

Her expression softened. "Then why wait now? It's just putting Eva at risk."

"You're right. We don't want Eva to suffer like your other patient. Like my friend."

"Right, my other patient. Well, I'd better get back to my game of poker. Eva cheats." She paused in the doorway. "I am sorry about your friend."

"Thanks," he said. "Okay, so I'll see you after your shift? Where should I pick you up?"

"The front doors. Though I hope you have space for my bike." She nodded and walked back into Eva's room.

There was a sadness about her. She'd obviously been affected deeply by her other patient to fight so strongly for Eva, to be so personally connected. And he couldn't help but wonder if the patient was someone close to Flo.

It was a close call. Flo didn't mean to let her emotions take control of her when they were talking about Ms. Martinez donating a kidney to Eva. She should've let him talk to her, not thought twice about it. It was Nate's prerogative as a surgeon to talk to his patients and make sure they were informed.

She shouldn't have let it affect her so much, but the problem was, it did. Eva reminded her so much of her own time in the hospital, and if her parents could've given her a kidney they would've. Only her parents, her brother and her sister hadn't been cross-matches. Her *năinai* had been, but she had been too elderly, so her kidney hadn't been viable for Flo.

So she'd sat on the list, waiting for some poor soul to die.

It was a great gift that anonymous person had given her, but it also weighed heavily on her. That's why she was trying to live life to the fullest. And Nate had lost a loved one who had been waiting on the list and she couldn't help but wonder who it had been.

It's none of your business.

It may not be, but it gave some connection to Nate that hadn't been there before. It helped her understand him more. He got it. Even just a little bit, he understood the emotions, fear and pain of this whole process. It just made him all the more attractive to her.

She shouldn't be going out with Nate tonight, but even though she was emotionally drained from their spat, she was intrigued.

He was taking her somewhere out of Los Angeles, somewhere she would have a lot of room to drive. She could tick it off her bucket list and, really, what did she have to lose? Seeing Eva chained to her hospital bed had brought back too many painful memories for her, and she'd lashed out, almost telling him that it was she who had been that girl, clinging to life while she'd waited on the transplant list.

And that wasn't anyone's business.

Thankfully, she had been able to convince Nate that it was a former patient of hers.

There was a roar of an engine and Flo glanced over to see a vintage Corvette screech around the corner and pull up in front of the building.

She smiled when she saw Nate get out of the driver's side of the car. "Well, what do you think?"

"Where in the world did you get this?"

"Believe it or not, it's mine. I keep it in storage here. For when I visit. Will it do?"

Flo laughed. "I think so. Will there be room for my bike?"

"Yep. We'll toss it in the trunk, it'll be fine."

Flo wheeled her bike over and Nate took it from her and secured it in the trunk. She noticed he wasn't dressed in his business casual clothes. Instead he was wearing denim jeans, biker boots and a tight, black V-neck shirt. His eyes were obscured by aviator sunglasses. He was a typical Californian bad boy. Or at least how Flo had always pictured them. She didn't have a lot of experience with the bad-boy type of man.

He was too damn sexy for her own good and she had to keep reminding herself that he was off-limits.

She climbed into the passenger side after Nate held open the door for her. Flo had never sat in a sports car before. That was something else she could check off her bucket list. Nate slid into the driver's side and turned the key, revving the engine.

"You ready?" he asked.

"I'm always ready," she said.

He grinned and then took off out of the clinic's loop driveway and out into the streets. Flo's hair, which had still been in a bun, blew out of it and whipped around her face as Nate drove through the streets of Los Angeles like a maniac.

When they stopped at a light Flo put her hair back into a tight ponytail. "I guess this is why women with long hair wear hats in these cars."

Nate chuckled. "Or scarves."

"I'm not wearing a scarf. Try not to drive like a lunatic."

"And what would you know about driving?" He revved the engine as the light turned green and then took off again toward the highway that led east out of LA and toward Vegas.

"You're not taking me to Vegas, are you? That's, like, six hours away!"

"No, it's in Barstow."

"Barstow! That's two hours from here."

"It's only four-thirty p.m. Do you have plans? I know for a fact you don't have an early shift tomorrow. You have a pretty decent one followed by a really nice dinner out."

She glared at him, but honestly she was glad for the car ride. She'd never been to Barstow. Heck, she'd never really been on a road trip. She'd always wanted to drive across the country. That was on her bucket list, as well. She wanted to drive Route 66 and hit every kitschy place she could. She also wanted to drive across the badlands and through Montana, Wyoming and maybe even up into Canada to Alaska.

She also wanted to do the drive in an RV and her family was *not* an RV type of family. Vacations were spent on a tropical beach somewhere, a place where Flo could rest and recuperate. A place of peace and tranquility.

Flo had had enough of peace and tranquility. She wanted to do things, see places. She wanted a collection of goofy postcards from places like the home of the world's biggest ball of string and Mount Rushmore.

Nate turned on the radio and Flo relaxed into the drive. She didn't have to say anything to him, she could just enjoy the sights of driving into the desert, watching the city trickle away into wide open spaces with the wind in her face and the sun at her back.

She forgot everything that had happened today, she forgot about her bucket list and limited time and for the first time in a long time she just relaxed.

"Hey, sleepyhead. Wake up."

Flo woke with a start and realized that she'd drifted off. The car was parked at a deserted drag strip and it was dusk.

And when she glanced at the dashboard she could see it was seven in the evening.

"How long was I sleeping for?"

"A couple of hours. You looked so peaceful I didn't want to disturb you."

"I'm so sorry."

Nate shrugged. "It's okay, but I thought you might want to *try* and drive a bit tonight before we have to turn around and head back to Los Angeles."

"Sorry." Flo got out of the car and stretched. "Where are we?"

"A buddy of my father owns this old drag strip. He's planning on refurbishing it, but he said we could come out here and practice driving around the parking lot. I'm not sure if he actually wants us to drive on the strip, though, so if drag racing is on that bucket list of yours..."

"It's not, meaning I've never really considered it."

Nate climbed out of the driving seat. "You ready to try your hand at driving?"

"Oh, yeah," Flo said, probably a little too eagerly. She

climbed into the driver's seat and did up the seat belt. Nate took her vacated spot in the passenger side. "What do I do first?"

Nate chuckled. "Turn the key in the ignition. That would be a good start."

"Ha-ha. I meant after that." She turned the ignition key.

"Whoa, don't jump the gun. Driving is an art form."

Flo snorted. "I find that hard to believe when any old schmuck can do it."

Nate rolled his eyes then placed her hands on the wheel. "Put your hands at ten and two and be quiet for a moment."

Flo stuck out her tongue. "What next?"

"Have you never been in the front seat of a car? Even fifteen-year-olds know this."

She grabbed the stick and put the car out of park into drive. It rolled forward a bit. "Which one's the gas and which is the brake?"

"Press it and you'll find out. Just gently."

"So no slamming?"

Nate arched an eyebrow. "Only on the brake, if needed."

"Okay." Flo pressed her foot down and the car lurched forward. She immediately jammed her foot down on the other pedal. "Whoa."

"There you go. Try again."

"Okay." Flo stepped down on the gas less and the car moved forward slowly. She smiled as Nate instructed her and she drove around the parking lot. Sometimes slow and sometimes fast, which caused Nate to shout out. But it was exhilarating.

She'd always wanted to drive, but her parents had refused to let her learn, even though by the time she was sixteen she had been two years post-op from her kidney transplant and doing well. She'd begged and pleaded, but her father had not relented.

"Why do you need to drive? We have a driver who will take you wherever you want to go."

Her parents had been so stubborn and then when she'd gone off to college and medical school, she'd never really thought about driving and had just been happy to take public transportation and not have a driver take her around.

Learning to drive was way down the bucket list, though it was something she had to do before she drove across the country. It was nice that Nate had faith in her and was letting her try and drive. No one else had ever suggested that to her.

Not even Johnny.

Don't think about him. This moment was just about friends doing something fun.

It was laid back and easy.

It was fun.

And it was only temporary.

Nate allowed her to drive around until dusk turned to darkness and a smattering of stars spread out across the sky. They grabbed a quick drive-through dinner then parked back at the deserted drag strip, lying out on the hood of Nate's car. Flo couldn't remember the last time she'd seen so many stars.

She had been young and it may have been once or twice when they'd been driving somewhere late at night in the country. The details were foggy, but she remembered the night sky being flooded with brilliant light, and that's what she could see now.

It was beautiful.

She glanced over at Nate. His arm was behind his head and he was staring up at the night sky with the same kind of wonder she was feeling. It made her heart skip a beat and she fought the urge to reach out and kiss him again.

It would be perfect if she did—kissing Nate under a star-filled sky—but she suppressed that urge and turned her gaze away. It was better that she didn't act on her impulse. There was no one else around. They didn't have to put on their act now. They were just friends.

And she wasn't even sure if they were friends, because she doubted she'd hear from him again once he returned to New York, and that realization made her feel sad.

"See, it was worth the drive, wasn't it?" he said, interrupting her thoughts.

"It was. You're right, this is great. I never see the sky like this in LA," she said with a sigh.

"It is. I used to come out this way with my dad. We'd find a campground out in the desert and watch meteor showers."

"Do your parents still live in Los Angeles?"

"No, they live in San Francisco. They love San Francisco and the lifestyle there. Why?"

"Just wondered. I mean, if they were here I'd ask why you're not staying with them."

"Would you stay with your parents if they were in town?"

"I wouldn't have a choice," Flo mumbled.

Nate chuckled. "Oh, really?"

"My dad grew up in Beijing and my mom in the deep south. They're quite overbearing and old-fashioned sometimes. They also drive me crazy."

"See, you wouldn't stay with them, either. Besides, maybe I have a bad relationship with my parents," he teased.

"Do you?"

"No," he said. "I care for them. I've just been so busy

in New York City. I never get to San Francisco. It's been a long time since I've been out this way. I forgot how much I love it out here. How I love the desert. I used to spend a lot of time out in the mountains when I was younger. I did a lot of rock climbing, too." Then his smile disappeared into a frown. "Well, that was a long time ago. I don't have time for that kind of stuff any more."

"I've always wanted to do rock climbing, or climb a mountain. Maybe Everest."

Nate shrugged. "It's hard work and dangerous."

"So?"

"It's on that crazy bucket list of yours, isn't it?"

"And if it is?" she asked.

Nate shook his head. "Why would you want to risk your life?"

"Life is meant to be lived."

"You can live your life without doing crazy things."

"What's the fun in that?" Flo teased.

"There's more to life than fun." There was a sadness to his voice.

"You okay?"

"Perfectly. Why wouldn't I be?"

"You sounded sad there."

"Not sad, just realistic. Well, we'd better get back to LA. Work tomorrow and dinner with potential investors." Nate slid off the hood and climbed back into the driver's seat. The moment was shattered and she blamed herself. Flo reluctantly got into the passenger seat. She didn't want to go back home to her lonely apartment. She wanted to keep driving. She wanted to spend the night on the hood of Nate's car, wrapped in his arms.

No. Not in his arms.

Nate was right. It was getting late and it was time to

head back to reality and LA. It was safer in LA, safer in her apartment far away from Nate.

"Thanks for tonight. It was fun," she said.

He smiled at her, but it wasn't the same easygoing, fun smile she was used to. It was subdued Nate again. "No problem. It was my pleasure."

Flo didn't say anything more to Nate as they headed west, back to the city, back to reality and back to the façade they were both very comfortable with.

CHAPTER SEVEN

"How much longer am I going to be holed up here, Doc? I'm supposed to start my stint on Broadway in five months. I have to prepare."

Nate glanced up from Kyle's chart. Kyle was sitting up in bed and doing better a couple days post-op from his LVAD surgery, but he still had a long way to go and even then he had an uncertain time ahead, hooked up to his machine as he waited for a new heart and lungs.

"I think it's in your best interests to cancel your stint on Broadway."

Kyle snorted and then winced in pain. "Are you crazy? This is a huge opportunity."

"One you'll have to pass up unfortunately." Nate crossed his arms. "You're hooked up to a machine. You can't leave the clinic. That machine is keeping you alive."

"The nurse said it was portable. She was having me walk around yesterday."

"Portable, but you still need to be monitored and you still need to be on oxygen a lot of the time. I don't see you tap dancing your way across a Broadway stage any time in the near future."

Kyle grinned. That famous smile that melted the hearts of many women, but which didn't work on Nate one bit.

He actually found it annoying more than anything else when Kyle tried to use that charm on him.

"There's no dancing. Besides, I could have a new heart and lungs tomorrow."

Nate pinched the bridge of his nose. "You could, but it still doesn't mean that you'll be up on your feet in a couple of weeks. You will be in the intensive care unit for a while, your body will have to heal from a long surgery, we'll have to monitor you for signs of rejection. It will be a long process of healing before you can return to the stage."

Kyle sighed and laid his head back. "I didn't ask for this."

"I know. I'm sorry."

"You paint a pretty bleak picture, Doc. At least that other doctor, at least she can give me some hope."

Nate frowned. "Was she the one who told you you'd be up on your feet in a short time?"

"No, she's just nice to look at." Kyle winked.

Nate laughed. "Thanks."

"Well, I don't have to tell you, right? I mean, I do keep up with gossip. You and her are a thing, right?"

Nate groaned inwardly. "Right."

"It's about time. You're always working; you never seem to have fun. I invite you to all my parties and you never come. Do you know how many beautiful women come to those parties?"

"I'm aware. Now, would you lie back and get some rest and either Dr. Chiu or myself will come in and look on you later."

Kyle grinned. "I hope it's Dr. Chiu. No offense, Dr. King, but I might just steal her out from under you."

"Sure you will. I'll see you later." Nate left Kyle's room and shook his head. Didn't people understand the severity of transplant surgery? They thought that once they had a new organ things would go back to normal. That they'd be able to do all the same things they'd been able to do before, but it was a huge lifestyle change. The chance of rejection in Kyle's case was high. Granted, it was getting better all the time with medical advances, but surgery was still the *practice* of medicine, which meant things weren't perfect.

If only they were.

If only organs could be grown from patients' tissues and blood. If only there wasn't rejection. If only...

Nate scrubbed a hand over his face. He hadn't had a moment to turn to his research since coming to Los Angeles and he was annoyed. When he was in New York his research was his companion at night and that was all he needed.

Since he'd landed back in LA, he hadn't even glanced at it. His nights had been filled with Dr. Florence Chiu and his days had been filled with prepping Eva Martinez and her mother for their kidney transplant surgery, as well as monitoring Kyle Francis, who was his top priority.

The thing was, he didn't really miss his research. He'd enjoyed the last couple of nights with Flo. Maybe because it was just temporary, there was no permanence to it and it made him feel safe. Since there was no permanence there was less chance of heartache.

The only problem was, he wasn't sure if he wanted to go back to the way his life had been before. Empty.

You don't have a choice.

Nate groaned as he noticed the time. He had to grab his suit from the office he shared with Flo and try to make himself presentable for this dinner, which was the last thing he felt like doing today. Especially when this wasn't even his place of employment.

He was just a locum surgeon, just passing through.

It's your own fault. You had to kiss her.

And he'd wanted to kiss her when they'd been lying out under the stars. Actually, any time he was around her he wanted to kiss her. It was maddening. It was distracting and he wished he could act on it, but he couldn't.

Nate placed the tablet he'd been using back on the charging station and headed toward the office. He'd brought in his suit so that he could make a quick change here and drive Flo to the restaurant in West Hollywood.

He just wanted to get this dinner and schmoozing over with as fast as he could. Then he could come back here and force himself to do some work on his research. His research was his life. There was no room for anything or anyone else.

When he got to the office Flo was already in there and already dressed in a suit, her long hair up and smooth, instead of the usual wisps that framed her face. His gaze was drawn to her long slender neck. She wore a red silk blouse and a tight black pencil skirt, with black heels, the kind that had a red sole.

She was absolutely stunning and he knew that this dinner was going to be a challenge.

Flo glanced up at him. "You're not dressed yet?"

"I was just coming to do that."

"Where were you?"

"Checking on Kyle." Nate peeled off his white lab coat and tossed it on Flo's couch. She frowned, moved past him and hung up his lab coat in the closet. He couldn't help but smile to himself. "You're such a neat freak."

"Actually, I'm not. Just in my office. I like my workplace organized, but at home my decorating style is *There appears to have been a struggle.*"

"Is that a style?" he asked.

"At my apartment it is. I don't have time to tidy it much. And I'm rarely there."

"I would've never pegged you for someone who would live in clutter."

"It's not a sty, it's just not as organized as it is here." Flo crossed her arms. "I can't believe you're not dressed."

"Chill, I brought my suit here. I'll just go into your bathroom and change." He opened the door and saw toothpaste smeared on the porcelain of the sink, scrubs wadded up on the floor and an abandoned hair straightener. There was also some lingerie on the floor. He chuckled and picked up the delicate lace with one hand. "It looks like your office bathroom has the same style as your apartment."

Her cheeks went beet red and she snatched the flimsy garment from him. "Would you get ready, for the love of all that's good and holy?"

Nate didn't argue any further. It wasn't worth it, because the gleam in her eyes brooked no argument. He quickly changed into his suit and cleaned himself up, mostly to get the smell of hospital off himself.

When he opened the door to the bathroom Flo was waiting for him. Her gaze raking him from head to toe and a finger thoughtfully tapped her chin.

"You clean up nice."

"Thank you, Dr. Chiu. You do, too."

She smiled. "Well, let's get this over and done with."

"I think we should swing by Kyle's room. Make him jealous."

Flo arched an eyebrow. "What're you talking about?"

"He's trying to move in on my territory." And then he realized what he'd said. He only hoped that Flo took it as a joke.

"Your territory?" she teased. "Since when have I been your territory?"

"Since the rooftop, or have you forgotten?"

She rolled her eyes and took his proffered arm. They walked out of her office together and he knew, as they walked through the halls of The Hollywood Hills Clinic, that everyone was watching them.

Usually that would make him feel a bit uncomfortable, because he didn't like to be associated with any woman. He didn't want rumors flying about him, but he didn't mind walking through the halls with Dr. Florence Chiu on his arm, and in those heels she was almost as tall as him. He could smell her hair. It was lavender.

There was a limo outside and Freya was standing outside. She waved when they walked over to her.

"I'm afraid I can't go with you tonight," Freya said.

Flo frowned. "Why not?"

"I'm needed somewhere else. I'm sure you and Dr. King can handle this dinner. Besides, it's you two the investors want to meet. They know me." Freya glanced at her cell phone. "I have to run, but the limo is yours and dinner is on the clinic. I've already talked to Dan Tana's. Everything is a go."

And before either of them could protest Freya was walking off in the other direction, texting someone.

"A limo. Wow." Flo walked over to it and the chauffeur opened the door for her. She slid in and as she did so Nate caught a glimpse of her thigh. It made his blood heat and he pulled at the suddenly tight collar of his dress shirt. All he could think about was being alone with her in a limo and how much room and privacy there was for the two of them. "Are you coming, Nate? It's great in here."

"Yeah." He took a calming breath and tried to chase those dirty, bad thoughts from his mind. The last thing he needed was to have an erection during a boring meeting with investors. Also because there was no way he could act on it. He hadn't planned on doing laps tonight at the pool, but now he was.

He had to seriously get a grip, but the more he tried to tell himself that the more his grip lessened.

Flo had never been to Dan Tana's. Actually, even though she'd been living in LA for a couple years, she really hadn't gotten out much. She didn't go to fancy restaurants, hadn't since she was a child, and she certainly didn't like investor meetings.

"You okay?" Nate asked.

"Why wouldn't I be?"

"Well, a moment ago you were pretty excited about riding in a limo and now you're stiff, on edge, like a rod is holding you upright."

Flo rolled her eyes and sighed, her shoulders dropping. "Fine. I don't like talking in front of crowds."

"Who said there will be a crowd?"

"Well, fine, a group of strangers. It makes me uncomfortable."

"You handled that press conference well," Nate said.

"No, I didn't. You did, though. I can speak to a crowd of doctors or nurses, anyone from the medical profession, but throw in people who aren't part of the medical profession and I just want to crumple up in a ball and cry."

Nate frowned. "That doesn't seem like you."

"How would you know?" She regretted the words. "I'm sorry."

He shook his head. "Fair enough. We haven't known each other long, but really it doesn't seem like you to be nervous like this."

"It is. Trust me." Flo began to tap her leg in agitation. "I have no idea what to say beyond 'Give us your money.'"

He reached out and put his hand on her knee to calm the tapping of her leg. It caused a zing of pleasure to race through her, his strong hand on her knee firing her senses. He moved his hand away. Her leg tapping had stopped and she was at ease.

Flo cleared her throat. "So what should I do? Do you have any suggestions?"

"Picture them naked."

Flo gasped and saw that devious twinkle in his eyes. He was joking with her. "You're crazy."

He shrugged. "There's nothing fundamentally different about talking to a press conference or investors. You're strong. You stood up to me the first day we met. Not many people have had the guts to do that."

"Why? You're not scary."

His brow furrowed. "Thanks for that."

"Why are you bothered by that?"

"You weren't scared when you met me?"

"No. Why would I be?"

"You just admitted large crowds make you nervous, but when you met me you weren't nervous?"

Flo felt her heart rate pick up speed. Of course she'd been nervous when she'd met him. He was gorgeous. He was the kind of guy who would never give a girl like her a second glance, so she'd been nervous when he'd stepped off that helicopter, looking so sexy. She just wouldn't admit it.

And she wouldn't admit that he made her nervous now, but in a much different way.

"No, I wasn't nervous. You're a surgeon, though, and only one man."

He frowned. "Most residents and interns are nervous

when they first meet me. They say I'm a bit of a monster. Cold. Detached."

"First, I find that hard to believe, and second, I'm not a resident. I'm a surgeon. I can deal with cold and detached. My father was a businessman, a CEO, and a lot of people feared him. My mom taught me to stand up for myself."

He grinned. "Then it should be easy to deal with a couple of investors. Just channel your inner dad and deal with them."

"You mean curse at them in Mandarin until they do what I want?" Then she laughed as she thought of her father. He'd tried for so long to get her to speak Mandarin, but she'd had no interest in learning it, except for the swear words.

He'd be horrified to know that's what she'd picked up in her endless classes in Mandarin. Of course, now she wished she had a second language under her belt and maybe that was something she could add to her bucket list.

"I think cursing at them will defeat the purpose." They shared a smile and the limo slowed down and stopped in front of the restaurant.

Flo took a deep breath and stared at the front of the restaurant.

You can do this.

"You can do this," Nate said, as if reading her thoughts.

"Maybe it shouldn't be me. Maybe it should be you."

He shook his head. "No, you're The Hollywood Hills Clinic's chief of transplant surgery. This is all you."

"Okay."

He nodded and opened the door, stepping out. Then he offered his hand and helped her out of the limo. As he held her hand he gave it a reassuring squeeze. It was exactly what she needed at that moment. A vote of confidence from someone she admired.

Yeah, she could do this. She had to do this.

They were whisked inside the restaurant, which was decorated in deep, rich colors, and the concierge led them to a large patent-leather booth in the far corner where the investors were waiting. As she walked through the restaurant she felt a hand in the small of her back as Nate gently guided her. It made shivers of anticipation run down her spine. To make matters worse, he looked so darned good in a well-tailored suit.

It was maddening.

"Ah, Dr. King and Dr. Chiu, I am so glad you could join us. I'm Cecil McKenzie."

"A pleasure to meet you, Mr. McKenzie." Flo shook his hand and Nate followed suit.

"This is Ian Brownstone and Travis Fleming," Cecil said, introducing the other two men at the table.

Flo shook their hands and then sat down, Nate and the rest of the men at the table sitting down only after she had.

"I have to say we were quite worried when your story leaked in the press," Ian said. "The Hollywood Hills Clinic prides itself on privacy and protection of their clientele."

"It was an unfortunate incident," Nate said. "Thankfully one that was unfounded as Dr. Chiu and I were in a relationship."

Nate was so smooth with the investors. He was obviously used to this. Flo was, somewhat, but only from watching her father schmooze clients in his business. Schmoozing was not her thing.

"Dr. King wasn't fully aware of the clinic's strict guidelines on privacy," Flo said. "He is from New York."

That got a bit of laughter from the men at the table.

"Well, we're glad to see that it's all been smoothed over and, honestly, it's been spun in such a good way. We're also extremely impressed with the pro bono case you've both taken on with Eva Martinez. Can you tell us a little bit about that?"

"Of course, The Hollywood Hills Clinic is working with the Bright Hope Clinic and Eva is one of hopefully many more children who will benefit from this initiative. You know, of course, that cases like this will bring in more positive press for paying clientele," Nate said.

And he continued to talk to the investors, winning them over.

Flo was trying to pay attention, but again this wasn't her forte and, frankly, bored the socks off her. She was pretty sure that these men didn't want to hear about the science behind the surgery and that's what interested her most.

Also the journey, because she'd lived it.

Only it was better they didn't want to know about the emotions. The struggles one faced when undergoing an organ transplant, because then she would have to tell Nate about hers and that was something she would never do.

That was her scar to bear alone.

As the salads were being taken away her cell phone began to buzz and it was long distance.

"Excuse me, gentlemen. No need to get up." Flo pulled out her phone and slid out of the booth, walking to a secluded, quiet spot by the bathrooms before she answered the call. "Dr. Chiu speaking."

"Dr. Chiu, I'm calling from UNOS regarding your patient Kyle Xavier Francis."

"Please go on."

"We have organs for him. We need you to come to San Francisco and retrieve them."

Flo's pulse thundered through her ears as the words sank in. This was the moment. The magic moment where someone was given a second chance, but also a moment of reverence because it meant the end of a life.

A brave soul who was giving the ultimate gift.

"I'll be there within the hour."

CHAPTER EIGHT

FLO FINISHED HER conversation with UNOS and then promptly called The Hollywood Hills Clinic to ready a chopper to take them to the airport and to have a chartered jet be readied to fly to San Francisco. She also ordered her team and the nurses to stop feeding Kyle and prep him for surgery. It was amazing luck to find a viable heart and lungs so soon. It was a relief. Then she cursed herself for being somewhat optimistic. She didn't know if the organs were viable. Not until she examined them herself.

Focus. Don't rush.

They had a little bit of breathing time as the surgery wasn't scheduled to start for another hour and the heart and lungs would be the last to be taken out, and she was going to be the one to do it. She was very particular about that.

She headed back to the table. Everyone stood up again.

"I'm very sorry to have to do this, gentlemen, but there is a medical emergency and Dr. King and I need to leave right away. I do apologize."

Nate glanced at his phone and she could see the text message there confirming the news she had just received. "Gentlemen, I'm sorry we have to cut this evening short."

"Of course," Mr. McKenzie said. "Don't worry about

us, and you can tell Ms. Rothsberg that we're impressed
and indeed interested in furthering our commitment to
The Hollywood Hills Clinic."

"Thank you." Flo shook their hands briefly and then
turned and walked away as fast as her heels would carry
her. The limo was called and it only took five minutes
for the car to pull up in front of the restaurant.

Nate told the driver to take them back to The Hollywood Hills Clinic.

"The chopper is waiting for us," Flo said, shaking her
leg in impatience. "Mr. Francis is fortunate."

Nate nodded. "He is. I'm glad you had your phone
on. I'm annoyed with myself that I put mine on silent."

"I never keep my phone on silent or I'd miss the calls
completely. I never know when it's vibrating."

They didn't say much else to each other. There was
nothing to say, because as soon as the organs were transplanted and Kyle was stabilized it would be the end of
their charade. Which was a shame, because Flo did enjoy
being around Nate. She liked working with him, too, but
they both knew there was a time limit on this act.

It was good that it would be over and done with. Then
she could get back to her normal existence. She could
throw herself back into her work and not think about
Nate so much, because she did. He also made her realize her loneliness.

And even though she hated to admit it, she was going
to miss him.

The limo had barely parked and Flo was out, kicking off her heels so that she could run through the halls
toward her office to throw on her scrubs and grab the
heart and lung machine that would keep the donor organs
alive and cool as they traveled back to Los Angeles. She
began to undress, with the door to her office barely shut.

"Whoa," Nate said.

She spun around, just in her red lace thong and bra with her shirt covering her torso. Then she realized what she was doing and covered her scar the best she could with her blouse. What had she been thinking? How could she have been so lax about it? She'd never changed in front of people. Not even when she'd been a surgical resident. She always found an excuse to slip away into a stall and change. She didn't want anyone to see her scar and think that she was weak when she wasn't.

Nate was looking the other way, but he was clearly uncomfortable. And she quickly turned around so her back was to him and slipped on her scrub top, dropping the blouse that had hidden her scar. She prayed he hadn't seen it. She didn't want to get into a discussion about her scar. There was no time for that and she didn't want him to know.

"What?" she asked.

"I wasn't expecting you to strip down."

Flo rolled her eyes. "Don't be immature. We don't have time."

She breathed a sigh of relief that he hadn't noticed her scar, but then she'd had her back to him as fast as she could when he'd walked into the room, plus she'd covered it with her blouse.

Why, though?

She was being chicken. Nate wasn't Johnny and he could handle seeing her scar. Why was she so scared about telling him? He'd said she was strong, and for a moment she'd believed him, but right now she didn't feel so strong. Not when she'd been so afraid of him seeing her so vulnerable.

Part of having her bucket list was being bold and brave. How could she be either if she hid the truth from the one person who might understand? Who wouldn't pity her?

Are you sure about that?

That doubt weasel in her head was stronger than she'd thought. It reminded her why it was better to be alone. To guard her heart like she'd been doing for so long. She couldn't go back to being hurt like that.

Still, she wished she could overcome her fear of people finding out about her illness. Maybe if she shared her experience then people would understand her deep connection and passion to saving those on the waiting list.

Maybe it would make her a better surgeon.

Maybe they would all pity you and question your abilities. Maybe they would think you were too emotionally attached to make a rational decision.

She shook those thoughts out of her head. "Are you going to get changed or what?"

"Fine." Nate shut the door and began to take off his clothes. First the suit jacket, which he tossed on the couch again, then the tie and the button-down blue shirt that brought out the color of his eyes.

Look away.

Only she was having a hard time trying not to look at him as she pulled on her scrubs. She'd seen him half-naked before, in tight swimming trunks, no less, with water running down his hard, tanned body.

Get a grip.

She pulled her hair up into a ponytail and grabbed her ID and jacket with "The Hollywood Hills Clinic" embroidered into it.

"I'm going to get the heart and lung machine. Shall I meet you on the helipad?" Flo asked, not looking at him as he kicked off his shoes and began to unbuckle the tight, tailored pants.

"Yep."

Thank goodness.

She snuck a quick glance at his tight backside and then shut the door, heading back up to her floor. When she got up onto the transplant floor, it was like a madhouse as people were scrambling and getting ready for the big show.

Flo stopped at Kyle's room. There were nurses hovering around him, more than usual. He saw her in the doorway and smiled.

"Do I understand there are organs for me?"

Flo nodded and walked toward him. "Yes, but remember, if they're not viable..." She couldn't even finish that sentence. She'd been over this with Kyle before.

He nodded. "I know. This could be one of those false starts you were talking about."

Flo squeezed his foot under the blanket. "I'm going to retrieve them with Dr. King. As soon as we land at LAX they'll wheel you into surgery. Dr. King will work on you, removing the LVAD, and put you on bypass."

Kyle held up his hand. "I understand. I'm more than ready, Dr. Chiu."

She smiled. "I'll see you in a bit."

A nurse handed Flo Kyle's chart on a tablet that was charged, and the means to transport the organs back. Flo took a deep breath and headed up to the rooftop. Nate was pacing and the helicopter was waiting.

It reminded her of the first moment she'd seen Nate, only this time they were riding off together and together they would save this man's life.

"You ready?" Nate shouted over the roar of the helicopter's blades.

"Ready."

He helped her load the equipment onto the chopper

before they got in. As soon as they were belted in the helicopter rose from the helipad and headed out over Los Angeles towards LAX, where the private jet was on the runway, waiting for them.

They didn't say a word to each other, not that they could've heard much over the noise of the blades. And when they were seated in the plane, they didn't say much either that didn't involve Kyle's surgery and the organ retrieval surgery. Flo would be the lead retrieval surgeon on the heart and lungs. She would hand the organs over to Nate, who would make sure they stayed stable and viable on their trip back.

Flo didn't mind. She didn't feel like talking.

She needed to keep focused on the task at hand and sent up a silent prayer for the lives that were being saved by this one person. It's what she always did even though she wasn't particularly religious, but still something she did.

When the plane landed there was an ambulance ready and waiting to whisk them off to the hospital, where the organ retrieval had started only ten minutes previously. Right now they were doing the laparotomy to make sure the organs were viable. If any organ wasn't viable then they could inform the surgeon who was retrieving the organ and the recipient could go back on the waiting list.

She fidgeted nervously as the ambulance raced through the San Francisco streets. She glanced over at Nate, who was absolutely comfortable. Or at least he appeared that way.

"You're not nervous?" she asked.

"Why would I be nervous? I've done this many times."

"What if the organs aren't viable?"

Nate sighed. "It would be too bad, but nothing I can stop. There's no use worrying about it. Why are you worried?"

"Because he's a big client. I wanted to do the laparotomy myself. I'm a bit controlling that way." That was part of the reason. She couldn't form the words and tell him that every time she went through the process she thought of the one time she'd gotten her hopes up and the organ hadn't been viable. The other kidney, which had gone to another recipient, had been fine, but the one destined for her hadn't.

And she almost hadn't survived her time on the waiting list again.

So she knew first hand what it would be like if she had to go back and tell Kyle that they couldn't retrieve his heart and lungs successfully.

When the doors to the ambulance opened, Flo jumped out and was ushered into the hospital by a resident, who took them straight through the hospital and to the ER. As she walked through the hospital she caught sight of a family.

A family in the waiting room.

A family that was grieving. They were holding each other up, mourning their loved one.

Her heart skipped a beat and for a moment she wasn't even there, because in her mind she was transported back to her own hospital bed, with hazy, tangled memories of her parents weeping and holding each other while she'd clung to life. The walk through the waiting room went in slow motion for Flo, her thoughts immediately going to her own donor.

She would never know who that person was, but if she did know she'd visit wherever they had been laid to rest and thank them.

Thank them for her second chance at life.

"Dr. Chiu?"

Flo shook her head and saw Nate was staring at her

with a concerned look and the resident was holding open the door to the OR floor.

"Sorry." She didn't glance back at the family. She couldn't.

She peeled off her jacket and hung it on a hook and then geared up, putting on a paper scrub cap and then scrubbing her hands. She glanced through the windows into the OR and saw the line of people waiting for organs.

"This will be fine," Nate said, scrubbing beside her.

"I know. It's just I don't like this part too much. I'm a surgeon and..." She couldn't even finish that sentence, because this was a life that wasn't being saved.

It was ending.

She preferred live donors. Like kidney, liver and sometimes lungs, when someone donated one lung to a loved one. There were rarely deaths in those retrievals. Those retrievals were done in love. There was a certain beauty to it.

There was a certain beauty to this moment as well, it was just that it had ended tragically for the donor.

She put on her mask and then headed into the OR, with Nate behind her holding one of the basins to collect the organs. She was gowned and gloved.

All she could do was wait. And she watched as organs were removed and people stepped forward to take them. They would be going off to different parts of the country. Saving countless lives.

"Dr. Chiu, we're ready for you now." The other surgeon moved to the opposite side of the table to assist. Flo stepped up. She closed her eyes and then went to work, but it didn't take her long. The bronchoscopy was done before the retrieval surgery to make sure that there were no signs of infection and the Gram stain came back clear.

It was now time to make sure that externally the lungs

were viable as the bronchoscopy only could see the lungs internally.

And as she carefully clamped and made ready to dissect she saw a dark spot. Her heart dropped to the soles of her shoes and she cursed under her breath as she felt the mass that grew into the pulmonary artery. She checked the heart and could see a minute dark spot beginning to grow.

Cancer.

Her stomach twisted in a knot and she tried not to be sick.

"I need to take a biopsy and I need it stat." If it wasn't cancer, maybe it was something benign and it would still be viable. She handed the specimens to the resident, who ran out of the OR to the lab.

Flo raised her hands, keeping them clean and rested while waiting, and tried not to curse. It couldn't be cancer. It just couldn't.

Nate came up behind her. "Dr. Chiu, what's wrong?"

"Look." She showed him the mass, the dark spots and where it spread.

Nate cursed, too. "Dammit."

Tears stung her eyes. If it had just been the lungs that were damaged, the heart could've gone to someone else. In Flo's case she couldn't take one and not the other, because it had to be one operation. Kyle's cardiopulmonary system couldn't stand the shock of two different surgeries. In his case it wasn't one or the other.

It needed to be both. The surgery had to happen at the same time.

Flo watched the clock, waiting for her answer. The donor couldn't be on bypass much longer. Even if the mass was benign, the organs would be useless if they were kept much longer where they were because the donor was missing other vital organs.

It was a race.

The resident returned. "I'm sorry, Dr. Chiu. It's stage-four lung cancer and the tumor originated from the heart. There's no record of any of it in the patient's file so it's highly likely the donor was unaware he had cancer."

Flo closed her eyes and cursed. "Thank you, Doctor. Would you please take the patient off bypass."

Dammit.

She tried not to cry.

The resident nodded and Flo began to close up the donor.

"I can do that," the resident said.

"No. I want to do it," she said, hoping her voice didn't crack with the emotion threatening to overtake her. She didn't want to explain to the resident why she felt the need to see this through. It was her way of thanking the donor for the ultimate gift.

A way to process the loss.

A way to thank her own donor for her life.

In fact, everything she did to advance transplant surgery was a thank-you, but, then, one could never thank someone enough for the ultimate gift. Except to live life to the fullest. The heart and lungs were not viable. She had been afraid of this, because it had seemed too good to be true. They hadn't seen it on the laparotomy because it had been on the other side and hidden. The mass hadn't infiltrated the lungs yet.

Nate had left the OR. She didn't even know he'd left, but he came back in now. "I called the clinic and told them to cancel Kyle's surgery."

Flo nodded and continued to work. When the monitors flatlined, she sighed.

I'm so sorry.

The apology was for this donor and for Kyle.

"Time of death twenty-two thirty-five." She pulled off her mask, not able to control the tears threatening to escape. "Doctor, can you finish closing for me? I have to get back to Los Angeles and my patient."

"No problem, Dr. Chiu." The resident took over and Flo dragged herself out of the OR, ripping off the paper mask and jamming it in the garbage can. Then she tossed off her gown and scrub cap, angrily throwing them into the receptacle before kicking it.

Dammit. It was so unfair.

"Whoa, what's gotten into you?" Nate asked.

"The organs weren't viable. What do you think has gotten into me?" Flo snapped.

"It happens, Flo. Why are you taking this so personally?"

Flo just rolled her eyes and began to scrub vigorously. "I'm not taking this personally. It's just frustrating."

Liar.

Of course she was taking this personally, because it had happened to her. And when it had happened to her she'd resigned herself at that moment to the thought that she was going to die. She'd been tired of fighting. No fourteen-year-old, no child, should resign themselves to dying.

She only hoped Kyle didn't.

She wanted to give him hope. It was just that right now she didn't know how.

At least the donor had saved countless other lives, just not her patient's. She finished scrubbing and they walked silently back out to the ambulance, the machine empty.

She was not looking forward to disappointing Kyle.

"I'll tell Kyle," Nate whispered, as if reading her mind.

"Thanks." Flo climbed into the ambulance, exhausted and defeated.

"I'm sorry you're taking this so hard," Nate said.

"Thanks."

"Think about all the lives that donor did save, though."

She smiled. "I know. I just feel bad for Kyle."

"He'll love it that you feel bad for him. He told me the other day that he's going to make a move on you."

Flo chuckled. "What?"

"That's what he told me. He really likes it when you come to check on him rather than me. He told me he was going to steal you away from me. Not that there would be any stealing on his part."

It was a sting, but it was the truth.

Nate wasn't hers and she wasn't Nate's. Still, it hurt all the same and she didn't know why she let it hurt. Nate couldn't be hers.

It was temporary.

She couldn't let Nate in. She couldn't risk her heart again.

"I'm afraid I'll still be disappointing him when I turn him down," Flo said.

Nate cocked an eyebrow. "Oh, really?"

"I don't date guys who have a broken heart." It had been meant as a joke, but Nate's smile disappeared like she'd hurt him.

"Right," was all he said, and didn't say any more.

An uneasy tension settled between them and Flo just let it be. She wasn't in the mood to discuss things further.

It was better this way.

It was better not to get involved and not to dig any deeper.

CHAPTER NINE

NATE KEPT HIS distance from Flo for a week. Even though he shouldn't have been bothered by her *I don't date men who have a broken heart* comment, it had stung. It had been meant in jest and if it had been anyone else he might've got a chuckle out of it, but Flo had been the one to say it.

It shouldn't bother him, because it's not like he was going to do anything about Flo, but it did, because he was slowly realizing he cared about her and that was scary.

How was she getting past his walls? He didn't know, but he decided after the failed transplant retrieval for Kyle Francis that it was best he stay away from her. So after disappointing Kyle and having a long talk with him, Nate threw himself back into his work at night. During the day he avoided being in the office. He found little corners to work in and the clinic had a nice research library tucked away on another floor.

At night, he worked on his papers and spent a lot of time swimming, but even then Flo's presence was there, and every time he got out of the pool he expected to see her waiting for him.

He had to get a grip and remind himself that there was nothing between him and Flo, but he did miss her companionship. He missed their friendship. And that's why he was now standing outside her office, hesitating about whether to go in. Only he had to go in. There had been some whispers about whether or not their relationship had ended or perhaps was on the verge of ending, because it seemed the dream team was drifting apart.

Freya had noticed and Nate had just come out of a meeting with her, having assured her that the distance was nothing. He'd just been working and things between Flo and him were fine.

As fine as they could be for a fake relationship.

"The door is unlocked."

Nate turned to see Flo standing behind him, grinning at him, a sparkle in her eyes.

"You have a way of sneaking up on people, don't you?"

"I do." Flo moved past him and opened the door to her office. "You know this is your office, too, so you're allowed to come and go when you want."

"I know. I was thinking and you interrupted my train of thought." He walked into the office and Flo followed, shutting the door behind her. She took a seat behind her desk and put up her feet on it.

"Well, I'm sorry about interrupting your train of thought. You've been busy. I haven't seen you around much."

"I've been working on my research.

"What is your research about again?"

"Mostly working on ways of regenerating organs and also the possibility of robotic replacements."

She arched her eyebrows. "I'm impressed, Dr. King. I've thought along similar lines, too."

"I figured as much. You're just as passionate about transplant surgery as I am." He cleared his throat. "I just got out of a meeting with Freya and I think we need to talk."

Her smile faded. "I think I know. I had that talk with her, too."

Nate nodded. "Something happened after Kyle's failed retrieval."

"Yeah, I took it too hard. I'm sorry for acting that way." Only she didn't look him in the eye when she said that and he couldn't help but wonder if there was something else going on there. Something she wasn't telling him.

It's not your concern.

"Okay, and I do understand. It was hard on me, too. Hard to break the news to him," he said. "Freya wants us to make some public appearances together before the big gala fundraiser tomorrow night."

Flo sighed. "Oh. I forgot about that gala. I hate getting dressed up for those things."

"The investors we had that brief dinner with wanted to throw a gala to raise money for the Bright Hope Clinic and raise awareness for donating organs. We kind of have to be there."

Flo wrinkled her nose. "I know."

"So, before that gala, I think we should go out tonight. Make a few public appearances so the press will stop printing stuff about us drifting apart."

"Drifting?" A blush crept up Flo's cheeks. "Tonight. Sure. What did you have in mind?"

"Surfing."

Her eyes widened. "Are you serious?"

"Is that on your bucket list?"

"No, actually, but it could be. It sounds like fun."

"I took a look at our schedules. We're both off at three and I think we should take a drive out to Venice Beach, because it's nearby and I can show you a few things."

"You know how to surf?"

"I told you I'm a native Californian. Of course I know how to surf. I spent many summers on Venice Beach. Plus it's a pretty safe activity compared to tackling Everest or letting you drive again."

Flo chuckled. "I don't have a bathing suit here with me."

He frowned. "Well, I'm sure you can pick up something along Venice Beach. I don't have one with me, either."

She rolled her eyes but smiled. "Okay. It sounds good. I guess I can't really say no to that, but I didn't really have you pegged for the surfing type."

"Why?"

"You don't seem to take a lot of risks. Don't take it the wrong way, but when I talked about mountain climbing, you seemed pretty against any kind of risk-taking."

"I had a friend, she took a lot of risks. Maybe some risks she shouldn't have."

Flo tipped her head to one side. "What kind of risks?"

"Riding a motorcycle without a helmet, for one thing."

"I wouldn't do that one. I'm not that much of a risk-taker."

Nate grinned. "You want to climb Everest."

"Have you?"

"No." Only he didn't tell her that it had been on his list once. Back when he'd done foolish things, taken chances and lived life to the extreme. Of course that had been a long time ago. Now he was a surgeon and understood the kind of trauma that could be done to a body doing those things.

He shook those thoughts out of his head and decided to change the subject.

"Surfing isn't too bad, as long as you don't do too much of it at dusk when the sharks feed."

She sat up straighter, her eyes wide. "Sharks?"

"You'll be fine. I have to do a round because I promised James I would, but I'll see you at the front in an hour."

He chuckled to himself as he left her office and then stopped, because again she'd gotten through his walls. She made him forget that he didn't do things like surfing or rock climbing or even traveling hours out of town to drive around a drag strip.

That was the old him. Someone he'd buried years ago. Why couldn't he have suggested dinner or a movie?

That's not you, that's why.

But it was. It had been for a while now. Or at least he liked to think it was him.

Nate scrubbed a hand over his face, angry at himself for being so weak when it came to Flo. He was angry at himself for allowing the man he'd once been to come back, because that's not who he was now.

That man was long gone.

Flo walked through one of the shops at Venice Beach that sold bathing suits. Or rather pieces of thread that seemed to be woven together loosely. At least for women. It was bad enough that she'd forgotten herself for a moment and stripped down in front of him once. Something she never did, because she didn't want anyone to see her scar. If they saw the scar, they either knew what it was because they were a surgeon or they asked questions that she was not prepared to answer.

Which was why when the sales assistant kept bringing her bikinis, which were ridiculously skimpy, she turned them down.

"I want board shorts and a top that will cover my abdomen. I'm going surfing," Flo said.

The shop assistant frowned. "But this would look cute on you."

"Maybe, but, please, I just want board shorts and a top. It's only April. It's cold still."

The shop assistant sighed and went off to dig some out. Nate had disappeared next door into the store that catered to men and where he could rent a couple of surf-boards for them. Hopefully he wasn't waiting for her.

"Oh, make sure it's not yellow. I heard that color at-tracts sharks."

"Oh, yeah," the shop assistant said, coming back with what looked like a one-piece wet suit. "Yum-yum yellow they call it on the Gold Coast in Australia. I learned that when I was studying over there."

Flo nodded. "Yeah, I definitely don't want to attract a shark."

"Well, this is a one-piece that is really popular with people who are looking for something more modest."

"I'll take it." Flo paid for it. "Can I wear it out?"

"Sure. The change rooms are in the back." The shop assistant handed her the bill. "Have fun."

"Thanks." Flo headed to the back of the store and quickly changed into the wetsuit. It was comfortable and most importantly it covered her scar. She packed her clothes in her bag and hurried outside to find Nate.

He was waiting beside his car, with two boards beside him and in a wetsuit, like her. Even though the wetsuit covered his gorgeous, muscular chest, it was tight in all the right places. He certainly filled it out well. Her cheeks heated and she tried not to think about the way he looked.

At least the scrubs at the hospital were loose on him. Shapeless.

Who was she kidding? He looked good in everything. It was almost criminal.

He smiled when she walked over to him. "Good choice, it's a bit chilly. It's only April after all."

"That's exactly why I picked it."

Liar.

She never really did think about the water being cold. Los Angeles was always warm and sometimes darned hot, but she didn't think about the water too much.

"You ready to go?" he asked.

"Just have to toss this in your trunk."

Nate opened the trunk and locked their stuff away, but pulled out a couple of towels.

"What're you going to do with your car keys?"

"My car is a classic. It was before computerized fobs." He pinned it to his wetsuit. "See no problem. Which board do you want?"

"As long as it's not yellow, I don't care."

Nate looked at her like she'd lost her mind. "You have an aversion to yellow?"

"Sharks like yellow."

"Who told you that?"

"I read something about it once. The shop assistant knew it, too."

Nate snorted and handed her a board that thankfully had no yellow on it. "Let's go then, you nut."

Flo stuck out her tongue and then jogged past him, the hot sand squishing through her toes as they headed toward the water. Thankfully there weren't many people out and about, so she wouldn't feel like such an idiot when she did a face plant or something.

She stood at the edge. The water was cold and lapped at her toes like it was taunting her. Nate set down his board and then knelt in front of her, his hands going around one of her ankles briefly.

"What're you doing?" she asked, startled.

"Proposing."

"What?"

"I'm adjusting your leash. The leg rope will keep your surfboard from being swept away if you fall, and you will fall."

"Thanks for the encouragement." She picked up her board.

"Have you ever surfed?" Nate asked as he wrapped the leash around his own ankle.

"No."

"Then you're going to fall. I haven't surfed in ages so I'll probably fall, too."

"I hope you do." And to prove her point she kicked some water at him.

"Hey!" He splashed her back, soaking her.

When she wiped the water from her eyes, he was already wading out into the water toward the swells.

What am I doing? What am I doing?

Yeah, she'd made a bucket list, but she hadn't done much about the bucket list. Though she had always had the intention of doing some of the stuff on it, her schooling and then her job had gotten in the way.

Maybe fear. Maybe Mom and Dad had been right. Maybe I shouldn't do this.

No. She wasn't going to chicken out. She'd spent her whole life being so protected and sheltered that she'd felt like she hadn't even really had a childhood. That's why she'd made the bucket list. She didn't know when her transplanted kidney might give up, but she had to *live*.

With determination she picked up her board and waded into the cold water after Nate, until she was beside him in waist-deep water.

"Glad you could join me." He smiled, that warm, charming smile that melted her heart.

"Let's do this. Show me how."

He nodded. "Okay, climb on your board. We're going to paddle out and then you're going to have to lift yourself up as fast as you can to ride the swell. Do you think you can do that?"

"I'll certainly give it a try." Flo took a deep breath and climbed on her surfboard, lying flat just like Nate.

She followed his lead, paddling out towards the swells. Thankfully they were small. She watched as Nate headed toward a larger one and, paddling faster, he leapt up with seeming ease and balanced as he rode the wave past her and toward the shore, before losing his balance and falling into the water.

Flo took a deep breath and aimed her sights on the next one. She did exactly what Nate had, paddling faster, and then tried to stand, only she couldn't. It felt like a ton of bricks was on her, and she got halfway up before the wave knocked her off her board into the water.

She surfaced, spitting water out of her mouth and rubbing it out of her eyes as she clung to her surfboard, which was now upside down.

Nate paddled toward her. "Good try. You almost got vertical there."

Flo groaned. "That was harder than I thought."

"I told you it's difficult. Do you want to stop?"

She grinned. "Not a chance."

They continued surfing until the sun began to set and she was absolutely exhausted, but that last time she stood on the board, albeit shakily, and rode the wave almost to shore, falling off in waist-deep water where Nate was waiting for her.

They picked up their boards and slowly carried them up the beach to where they'd left their towels. Flo sank down into the sand, using the towel to wipe the water from her face. Nate knelt down beside her, his blond hair plastered to his face, but it quickly began to curl in the warm breeze. He undid the leash on her leg.

"Thanks. My legs feel like Jell-O," Flo said. All she wanted to do was sink into the warm sand and sleep.

"You were awesome." He smiled up at her, making her heart skip a beat. "Better than Serena the first time I showed her."

Then his expression changed to something unreadable.

"Thanks." She could feel the blush creep up her neck. "Who was Serena?"

"A friend. She passed away."

"Was this the friend who was waiting for the organs?"

He nodded curtly. "Yeah, she's the one who lived dangerously, until she couldn't."

"Sounds like she lived life to the fullest."

"Yeah," he snorted. Something had changed. A moment ago he'd been relaxed and having fun with Flo, teaching her how to surf, and then something had changed when he'd started talking about Serena and her death. She couldn't help but wonder if Serena had been more than a friend, and that thought made her feel a bit jealous, when she really had no right to be jealous about who he had been with in the past.

If he'd even been with her.

Nate's past paramours, living or dead, weren't any of her business, as long as it didn't interfere with the facade that they were dating and had been dating for some time. That was the extent of her relationship with Nate, beyond a professional one, and she had to keep reminding herself of the fact. Though it was hard to when she found herself enjoying her time spent with him. She wanted to get to know him more.

"Well, thank you for taking me out there and teaching

me how to surf. Albeit badly. I really had fun," she said, trying to defuse the tension that had fallen between them.

"I'll take these back to the rental place and I'll be right back. Just wait here." He picked up his towel and dried off his face and hair, before picking up both boards with ease and walking back to the shop.

Flo let out a sigh of contentment and watched the sun set below the line of the ocean. The sky was full of brilliant oranges and reds. It was so nice out here and for one moment she forgot everything. She closed her eyes and listened to the waves lapping against the shore. It was calming. It made her think back to that one summer her family had spent on Whidbey Island and a particularly sunny day in the Pacific northwest. It had been one of the happiest moments of her life.

One stolen moment from her childhood that her family had had. They'd had fun and had forgotten that she'd been so sick. It was like they had just been a regular family. Not a family constantly going from the hospital to work, to home. She opened her eyes to see the sun had set completely. She hadn't realized how long they'd been surfing and her stomach growled in hunger.

"Bring your towel, Flo, and we'll rinse the salt water off."

Flo turned around and saw Nate. Her breath caught in her throat at the sight of him. He'd unzipped his wetsuit and bared his muscular chest, his wetsuit hanging around his slender waist. The afterglow of the sunset made his tanned skin glow like he was a bronzed god.

Think about something else. Quick.

Only she couldn't.

"Okay," she said, hoping there wasn't a tremble in her voice. She grabbed her towel and followed him to the showers against the surf shop where he'd rented the boards from. He pulled the cord and fresh water started raining down; she just watched him, mesmerized.

She shook off all the naughty thoughts that were going through her head and pulled the cord on the shower next to him, but nothing happened.

"It's not working?" he asked.

"Apparently not," she said, trying not to look at him. "I'll just wait until you're done."

"Don't be silly." And before she could say no he was pulling her under the water with him, their bodies close together. He ran his large strong hands over her, rinsing the sticky salt water from her body. Then he undid her ponytail, running his fingers through her hair, and she was frozen.

Her pulse roared through her body as he touched her.

No one had ever touched her like that.

No one else had run their fingers through her hair.

Then his hands came around and cupped her face, forcing her to look up at him. She realized how much he towered over her. His expression was unreadable but intense. It felt like time was standing still as she gazed up into his deep blue eyes. The water had shut off and the encroaching darkness caused the droplets of water in his hair to sparkle.

Kiss me.

Only she couldn't let him do that. It wouldn't be right, no matter how much she wanted another kiss, because she knew that kiss would lead to something more.

And she wanted that something more.

She wanted that night of passion.

Desperately. But it wouldn't be a smart move.

She broke the connection and stepped out of the shower, wringing her hair out. "That was great."

Nate cleared his throat. "Yeah, that was fun. I should take you home."

"That would be good." She picked up her towel and slipped on her flip-flops.

Nate did the same, wrapping the towel around his neck, but as they walked back to his car he took her hand. It sent a shiver of delight through her.

"What're you doing?" she asked.

"There's paparazzi here," he said in an undertone. "It's why I brought you into the shower with me."

And then she saw them out of the corner of her eye.

The shower had all been an act. The connection she'd thought they had hadn't existed. And even though it was for the best, it hurt all the same.

CHAPTER TEN

"Now, there's the hot doctor the whole entertainment world is talking about this morning!"

Nate shook his head as he walked into Kyle's room at The Hollywood Hills Clinic. Kyle was looking worse and the left ventricular assist device was starting to take its toll on him faster than Nate liked. Now Kyle sported a nose cannula and was on extra oxygen support twenty-four hours a day.

"I can't say that I'm flattered that you're calling me a hot doctor, Kyle."

Kyle snorted. "Please. As if. It's in the papers."

"What?"

Kyle tossed a trashy magazine at him and Nate picked it up to see pictures of him and Flo surfing. The caption said: *Kyle Francis's Doctors Get Hot and Heavy.*

And the caption wasn't wrong. He tried to tell himself that he'd pulled Flo under the same shower as him because he had seen paparazzi taking pictures of them. He'd done it as a stunt, but then, when she'd been so close to him, she'd aroused him.

She'd burned his very soul.

Before he'd known what he was doing, he'd been undoing her ponytail and running his fingers through her hair. He'd wanted to kiss her. Badly. But that would have been very bad, because if he'd acted on his impulse he wouldn't have been able to stop himself from making love to her right then and there.

He didn't like this loss of control. If he lost control, well, he didn't want to think about it. That carefree risk-taker he'd once been was long gone.

"She's really sexy," Kyle said, interrupting his thoughts. "You're a lucky guy. She's smart, too."

"Thanks," Nate muttered, suddenly feeling very jealous that a man like Kyle was calling Flo sexy.

So? She's not yours.

He shook those possessive thoughts away. "I came to check on how you're doing."

"How I'm doing?" Kyle asked. "Seriously?"

"Kyle, you've got to hang on. I know it's tiring…"

Kyle sighed loudly. "You know it's tiring? Do you? Have you ever waited for an organ?"

"Technically, yes. I've been waiting for yours for some time."

Kyle rolled his eyes and chuckled. "I guess you have. I'm trying my best, Doc. I'm trying."

Nate squeezed his shoulder. "I know you are."

"So what're you up to tonight?"

"Are you asking me on a date, Mr. Francis?" Nate teased.

"As if. Well, I guess sort of. You going to visit me tonight and keep me company?"

"I can't," Nate said. "Dr. Chiu and I are heading out to a gala tonight. I have to go rent a tux."

"Rent?" Kyle asked, horrified.

"Yes. I don't have my tuxedo with me. I wasn't prepared to attend any big parties out here."

"Pass me my cell, Doc."

Nate picked up the phone and handed it to Kyle. Kyle punched in a number.

"Hey, Martin. It's Kyle. Yeah, I'm good, man. Look, I need a favor. My doctor needs a tuxedo for tonight. He's about my size. I know I have something in my wardrobe. Can you bring a few of my choice ones from the last couple of award shows and we'll get him fitted. Great. Thanks, man." Kyle ended the call. "All taken care of, Doc."

"Who was that?"

"My personal assistant, Martin. Look, I never wear the same tuxedo to an award show or movie premiere twice. Usually at the end of the year I just donate them or give them to charitable auctions. They just sit there. I want you to have one."

"Thanks, Kyle. I really appreciate that."

"No problem. I'll have a nurse page you when Martin gets here and you can do a dying man one wish and show me which one you pick. Also, I would really like to see a picture of Dr. Chiu all dressed up."

"Yeah, that's never going happen, dude."

Nate turned to see Flo walk into the suite. She was smiling warmly at Kyle. "How are you today?"

"Dying apparently," Nate said.

Flo crossed her arms. "Kyle, we'll find you organs."

"I know, but can't I just milk that a little bit?" Then he flashed her that smile that melted the hearts of women everywhere. "Don't you have pity for me, Dr. Chiu? Just a bit?"

She rolled her eyes. "No one gets to milk anything around here. Haven't you heard the nurses refer to me as the difficult surgeon? I'm hard as nails."

"Somehow I don't believe that," Kyle said, grinning at the both of them.

Flo checked his vitals. "Well, Dr. King will see you

later and maybe if you're good I'll swing by in my dress. I'm getting ready here because the clinic is providing limos for everyone. So I'll take advantage of the free ride."

"Smart move." Kyle lay back down, looking exhausted.

"Get some sleep," Nate said. "I'll see you later."

He and Flo walked out of Kyle's suite and Nate shut the door.

"What do you think, Dr. King?"

"I think he needs organs sooner rather than later. He's not doing as well on the left ventricular assist device as I would've hoped."

She jammed her hands in the pocket of her lab coat. "I know. The LVAD gave his heart more time, but it's putting pressure on his lungs. They're deteriorating fast. I don't want to intubate him, his other organs wouldn't handle it for long. His chance for compartment syndrome and multi-system organ failure is high. Higher than I'd like."

Nate sighed.

Dammit.

Kyle was a nice guy. He may have been a world-famous superstar actor, but he was also a decent human being. He was in his mid-forties. That was too young to die all because he was on a waiting list.

Waiting.

Yet that's what had happened to Serena. Her injuries had been so extensive the only thing that might've saved her had been a new heart, but one hadn't become available, because she'd been so injured that the chances of her surviving a heart transplant had been low.

Then she'd gone into multi-system organ failure and she had gone before he'd even had time to process it all.

"You're thinking of your friend?" Flo asked gently.

"Why would you assume that?"

"Your expression. I may not have picked up my dad's flair for talking to a bunch of businesspeople, but I did pick up his knack for reading others."

Nate sighed. "You're right. I was thinking about her. Kyle's situation reminds me a bit of hers. I hate seeing Kyle suffer. I hate seeing him wait and slowly die when I know what the solution is. I could save him, but I'm missing two key ingredients."

"I know. Me, too. It's difficult waiting and feeling so helpless."

"Yes, helpless. I don't like that feeling very much."

"At least we can save one life tomorrow evening," Flo said.

"Eva?"

Flo nodded. "Everything is green lighted. It's time, and Ms. Martinez is ready and everything has been cross-checked. We're going to do the operation tomorrow night, because of Ms. Martinez's insurance."

"Okay. How is Eva doing?" he asked.

"She's good. She's scared and rightfully so, but I'm confident about this surgery. I did another MRI on Ms. Martinez, just to be on the safe side, and her kidneys are fine. I suggest you take the left kidney over the right."

"Sounds good."

Flo glanced at her watch. "I'd better run. Have some more rounding to do before the gala tonight. Shall we meet back up at Kyle's suite before we head down to the limo?"

"I thought you said to him, 'That's never going to happen, dude.' Changing your mind and wanting to impress the Hollywood actor?"

She laughed. "No, just letting him milk his situation a bit more."

Nate chuckled. "Okay. I'll see you here at four. That gives Kyle time to give us his best pointers for the gala."

She nodded as she walked backwards down the hall. "Right."

Nate ran his hand through his hair and headed back to the research library. He needed some time by himself, to collect himself before this gala. He was going to need all his wits about him to survive this and he certainly wasn't looking forward to wearing Kyle's tuxedo or trying on a bunch of tuxedos in front of him.

That wasn't his thing, but it was better than a rental.

At least now he didn't have to leave the hospital.

"I think that's the one, Martin. What do you think?"

Nate adjusted the cuff links and straightened the sleeve of the designer tuxedo Kyle had given him.

"I think so," Martin said. "It's the best fit. That's the one you wore last year."

Nate cocked an eyebrow. "Did you win an award in this one?"

"I did." Kyle chuckled and then waggled his eyebrows suggestively. "So it's a lucky tuxedo, too, if you catch my drift."

"I've been treating you for three years, Kyle. I *always* catch your drift." He glanced in the mirror in Kyle's luxurious private bathroom and straightened his bow tie.

Yeah, he could do this. He was uncomfortable, but it was just one night. He'd seen Flo dressed up before and this would be no different.

"Your date is here," Kyle called out.

Nate stepped out of the bathroom and then stopped in his tracks. He was not prepared for the visual assault to the senses that was waiting for him. He'd prepared himself to see Flo in a dress, but he hadn't quite prepared himself for this.

To have his breath completely and utterly taken away by her.

She looked a bit uncomfortable, standing in Kyle's suite. Her black hair swept up and off to the side, but it was the dress that caught his attention as his gaze hungrily devoured every inch of her.

Her dress was gray and flowing, with burn-out lace over top of it. The bodice was sheer with the lace strategically placed over her firm breasts. She spun around and her back was bare.

"What do you think, Doc?" Kyle asked.

Nate only briefly glanced at Kyle, who was grinning from ear to ear like a Cheshire cat. Normally Kyle's smugness about Flo would've bothered him, but he didn't care about Kyle or Martin or anyone else in the room.

He only had eyes for Flo.

And he knew at that moment he was a lost man.

Flo was shaking like a leaf; she only hoped that Nate didn't notice how nervous she was. She wasn't sure about the dress, but Freya had been the one to help her pick it out. She'd never worn anything so revealing before in her life.

She'd never gone to prom, so she'd never really dressed up.

Not that her parents would've approved if she had been asked by someone to go to prom. So this was her first real time getting dressed up to the nines.

Nate also made her nervous, because when he'd stepped out of that bathroom she hadn't been quite expecting a tuxedo or how *good* he looked. She'd seen him in a suit before, but there was just something about a designer tuxedo that made her heart beat a little bit faster.

"Well, what do you think?" she asked. "Is it too much for the event?"

"No. Not too much," Nate said. He walked over to her and took her hand in his, causing a shiver of anticipation to race through her. "It's perfect. You look…stunning." He brought her hand up to his lips, placing a kiss against her knuckles, which made her blood ignite in flames. She knew from that moment she was doomed.

"Thank you," she whispered, finally finding her voice.

Nate took her arm. "Shall we?"

"Okay," she answered, feeling like everything she was saying sounded dumb.

"Have fun, you two!" Kyle called after them. "If I wasn't laid up in this bed, Doc, you know I'd be stealing Dr. Chiu from you, so you'd better—"

Flo didn't know what Kyle was going to say as the door shut behind them. Nate was grinning and she couldn't help but laugh.

As they headed to the front, where a fleet of limos was waiting for those who were going to the gala, Flo caught sight of Freya, James and Mila standing there, waiting for Flo and Nate to arrive.

Freya covered her smile with her hand, her eyes gleaming with pride. She moved her hand and mouthed, "You look beautiful," to Flo. Even James was looking at her appreciatively.

Nate led Flo outside. They had their own private limo—the surgical dream team heading to the big gala that would raise money for the Bright Hope Clinic and many more transplant surgeries.

So it was only fitting that Flo and Nate arrived separately from the other people from The Hollywood Hills and Bright Hope clinics, and that made Flo feel like a bit like a Hollywood starlet.

The chauffeur opened the door and Nate helped Flo climb into the back. She adjusted her skirt and Nate climbed in beside her. The door shut and they were alone, except for the chauffeur behind the privacy screen.

Nate reached down and picked up her hand, holding it, his thumb circling the pulse point on her wrist, making her catch her breath just a bit.

"Kyle has good taste in tuxedos," she managed to say finally.

Nate glanced down and ran his free hand over his lapels. "Yeah, well, this is designer and apparently this is the tuxedo he won an award in last year."

Flo gasped. "You mean for *It's an Honest Truth*?"

"I guess so. I haven't seen that movie. Have you?"

"I have. It's a beautiful movie about the underground railroad. It made me bawl like a baby."

"I'll have to watch that," Nate said.

"Maybe we can watch it together later."

He grinned. "Maybe another day. Tonight I don't plan to watch much television. We do need to get a good night's rest for Eva's surgery tomorrow."

Flo nodded. "You're right."

For one moment she thought he was suggesting something else and she held her breath, but then again why would he? This was all an act. He'd made that clear the other night at the beach. But if he wanted to make love to her, she wouldn't stop him.

Act or not, for once she wanted to taste that forbidden passion. She wanted to know what it was like to take a man in her arms and feel that moment of connection. She wanted to experience what it was like to make love to a man. And she hoped they'd still be able to have that after she told him and everyone else how important transplant surgery was to her.

Nate had lost a loved one. He'd understand.

Flo couldn't hold it in any more. If she was going to give herself to Nate there would be no way to hide her scar. She had to be brave. She had to tell him that she was the recipient of a donor kidney. She'd almost died waiting and that was why she wanted to live life to the fullest.

It was time to be brave.

Nate was not Johnny.

She could do this. The bucket list was nothing if she continued to hide and not act boldly. Taking risks and doing some crazy things were one thing, but how could she be true to herself if she was terrified to keep hidden a part of her that she was proud of?

That was no way to live any more.

And Flo wanted to live. She wanted to feel.

And have a man make love to her. She couldn't think of a better person than Nate. She trusted him, she'd grown to like him, and even though nothing would ever come of their one night together, she could have that stolen time.

They didn't say much else to each other. The drive to the iconic Beverly Hills Hotel was brief. Soon the chauffeur was opening the door to a red carpet. There were flashes from cameras as Nate helped Flo out.

The investors and The Hollywood Hills Clinic had gone all out, making it a red-carpet event. The whole hotel had been rented for the night. Freya had told her that everyone would have a room, so no one would have to drink and drive.

Of course, that wouldn't be an issue for Flo. She didn't drink. She couldn't because of her transplant. Alcohol would be destructive for her kidneys and that was one thing she didn't mind missing. She had no desire to experience it.

Still, she might stay at the hotel, because when else would she be able to experience the opulence of old Hollywood by staying at a Los Angeles icon?

Nate placed his hand on the small of her back. This time, though, her back was bare and the brush of his hand on her skin made her gasp slightly. It burned even though it was hot out, but it burned in a different way. A way that made her body flush and tremble. He ushered her past the throng of press to the staging area, where couples were able to pose for their picture to be taken in front of a wall of sponsors' names.

Flo smiled as Nate put his arm around her and they posed for the camera. The surgical dream team. A force to be reckoned with.

Once their photo had been taken they were ushered into the hotel and led to the ballroom. When they entered it took Flo's breath away. On the ceiling there was a chandelier made of thousands of white flowers and twinkling lights.

There were flowers everywhere. White and sparkle lights filled up the ballroom. It was the most elegant thing she'd ever seen. They were shown to their table and took a seat with their investors.

The dinner was sumptuous, but all she could focus on was being in this amazing place with Nate by her side. He often took her hand. Champagne was poured, but she kept to water, even though there were a few curious glances. But she didn't care, because in a few moments she was going to get up there and ask a ballroom full of the rich and famous to give money to their charity and implore people to donate their organs, and she was going to tell them all why.

She was tired of hiding her kidney transplant. She never had before a man she'd loved had run from her because of it.

So Nate would soon know and she was okay with that. He was leaving anyway, but she couldn't hide it any more. He needed to know.

She wanted him to know, because maybe if then they connected in some way deeper than that moment she gave herself to him, it would mean so much more.

"Thank you all for coming here tonight," Freya said, getting the attention of everyone. "The Hollywood Hills Clinic is pleased to team up with the Bright Hope Clinic. It is our hope to continue to help this fantastic organization bring health care to those less fortunate."

There was a round of applause.

"Our first transplant operation with the Bright Hope Clinic is to help an underprivileged girl receive a new kidney, and to talk more about organ donation I am very pleased to introduce The Hollywood Hills' chief transplant surgeon, Dr. Florence Chiu."

Flo took a deep breath and stood up, making her way through the tables toward the stage. Freya stepped down and Flo was alone up there. The lights blinded her from those in the audience, but in the crowd she only saw one face. She focused on one person.

Nate.

"Hello, I'm Dr. Florence Chiu and I run the transplant surgery team at The Hollywood Hills Clinic. I'm also an organ recipient." Her breath was shaking and tears were threatening to spill down her cheeks, because it had been so long since she'd uttered those words without fear of retribution or even her own fear of admitting that her time was limited.

"I was born prematurely, and because of that I always

had health struggles. But when I was ten I collapsed and the doctors discovered my one functioning kidney was failing. I underwent years of dialysis as I sat on a waiting list. I had a couple of my own close calls, thinking that I was about to get a viable organ, only to find out that either the cross-match was negative or the organ wasn't viable.

"When I was fourteen, while I was lying in a hospital bed in Seattle, my time was almost up when my surgeon got a call from UNOS. A young man had died during a car accident, but he was an organ donor and his cross-match was almost perfect with me.

"Because of that young man filling out his donor card I'm here today, imploring you all to do the same. Because of him, I'm alive. I've been given a second chance and I chose to become a surgeon and help others like me. Like Eva. Medical professionals work hard to save lives, but you can save countless lives by donating your organs after your death. Also please think about donating financially to the Bright Hope Clinic and the amazing research that's being done in the name of transplant surgery. Hopefully one day donors won't be needed and lives can be spared while on the waiting list. Thank you for your time and enjoy your evening."

It was silent for only a moment, but then there was thunderous applause and a standing ovation, which made her cry, just for a moment.

She glanced over at Nate and he was standing, a smile on his face as he applauded her. There wasn't a sign of him feeling uncomfortable, or of him leaving because her future was so uncertain. He was still there and nodding his head in agreement.

He wasn't leaving and, best of all, he didn't look at her with pity.

There was no pity there.

She walked off the stage and shook hands with Freya, Mila and James, and then stood in front of Nate. He took her hand and kissed it again. Music started, because the dinner was over, and people began to drift out onto the dance floor.

Nate didn't say anything to her as he led her out to join them. People clapped as he spun her round and then pulled her close against him, his hand on her back.

Her knees were knocking together as she danced with him. So close to him. Her pulse raced and their gazes locked. The rest of the room was a blur to her, her only focus Nate.

All she saw was him. And she prayed her admission didn't drive him away.

"So that's why you don't drink."

She nodded. "That's why."

"Why didn't you say anything before?"

"Because I didn't want your pity."

"I don't pity you. There's only admiration here. I admire you," he whispered against her neck, making her body quiver with desire and relief. He was the first man who hadn't pitied her. Everyone pitied her.

Flo tried to swallow the lump in her throat, tears welling in her eyes. She didn't want to cry. Not now.

"Thank you," she said, finding her voice again.

"You make sense to me now," Nate said. "Before, you were so hard to figure out, but now… I get why you were so frustrated when Kyle's organs weren't viable. You've been there."

"I have."

He nodded. "You share my pain. Though it was a loved one I lost. I didn't almost lose my life."

"You still lost."

"I don't feel like I've lost at this moment," he whispered. "Being here with you, I feel...I feel like my old self again."

Her heart raced, adrenaline and desire coursing through her. If she didn't do this now, she might never do it. "I don't want to talk about that right now." And before he could say anything else she kissed him, but this was more than the featherlight butterfly kiss that she'd stolen from him when they'd been outside his hotel.

This was more.

This kiss was an invitation for him to take her, because what she wanted more than anything was to be with him. She wanted him to make her forget about her transplant, make her forget that she'd spent so many years sick and sitting on the sidelines.

Right now, she wanted to live.

He resisted at first, but only for a second, then his mouth opened against hers. His arms went around her, lifting her up on tiptoe as he deepened the kiss. His hands were hot on her bare back, holding her tight against him.

She'd never wanted someone as badly as she did Nate.

The kiss ended and she could barely catch her breath, her body quivering with desire. He rested his forehead against hers.

"Flo," he whispered.

"No, don't say anything." She took his hand and led him off the dance floor. No one was paying attention to them any more as people mingled, drank, danced and bid on the silent auction items. It was a perfect moment to lead him out of the ballroom to the elevators. She pulled the card she'd been given out of her wristlet and swiped it to summon the elevator.

Nate took her in his arms again and kissed her, pressing her against the wall next to the bank of elevators, grinding his hips against her, letting her know exactly just how much he wanted her. And the fact that he wanted her that much made her feel faint.

He wanted her, just as much as she wanted him. If they weren't wearing so many clothes, if they weren't in a public place, she would have had him right here and now, but she wanted this to be slow. She wanted to savor this time, because this wasn't permanent.

It couldn't be permanent because of her medical issue.

So she was going to enjoy this moment. They got on the elevator and her pulse was racing as they rode up to where her room was.

This was really going to happen.

The elevator dinged and she pulled him out into the hallway. She was nervous as she led the way to her room. She opened the door and flicked on the light, just one. The door shut behind them and she was suddenly very aware of him so close to her.

A tingle of anticipation ran through her.

"Florence," he whispered, using her full name.

"Nathaniel." And that was all she had to say and she was in his arms again. Kissing him. No words were needed, because she knew they both wanted the same thing. She stood in front of the bed and he was behind her, undoing the clasp on the back of her gown, the small piece of sheer fabric that held her dress up at her neck and the hook at her waist.

Once the dress was undone, he ran his hands slowly over her shoulders, pushing the dress down and off.

"So beautiful," he murmured, pressing a kiss on her shoulder. His hands skimmed over her again, and he drew the dress down over her hips so that she was standing in a pool of fabric, wearing only her slip and heels. She hadn't worn a bra because her dress had been sheer.

She was vulnerable to him and that would've scared her before, but suddenly it wasn't scary for her. It was all too real.

And she wanted it. She pulled off her slip.

He gently turned her around and her hands instinctively went to the scar on her lower abdomen, but he grabbed her wrists and held them, stopping her from covering up the scar, like she'd done before. Like she'd been used to doing. She'd thought it was so hideous, a blatant reminder to the world of her weakness. That she'd been sick, that she wasn't perfect. Then again, who was perfect?

"You don't need to hide it from me." He dropped to his knees and placed a kiss against the scar, catching her off guard. "This is part of you. This is what makes you strong."

And when he said those words a tear did escape her eye and roll down her face. No man had ever made her feel so beautiful, so wanted as Nate did right now. He stood back up and held her close in his arms. He brushed the tear from her face with his thumb.

"Don't cry."

"I usually don't, but I can't help myself around you."

"You're strong. Stronger than I thought."

He kissed her again. It was urgent against her lips as he drew her body tight against his. She began to undress him, because there was no turning back for her. First she peeled off his tuxedo jacket, then worked on the bow tie so she could get to his shirt buttons. She wanted them open so she could feel his skin and run her hands over his chest.

He took her hands and held them in his own and then kissed her again. A kiss that seared her down to her very soul. Their bodies pressed together and warmth spread through her veins, then his lips moved from her mouth down her body to her breasts.

She gasped in surprise at the sensation of his tongue on her nipple. Her body arched against his mouth and the pleasure it brought her. She'd never experienced anything like this before. Even though she was a virgin, she'd made out with a man before and it had never fired her senses so.

"I want you, so much," she said, and she was surprised that she'd said the words out loud, but it was the truth. She started to pull him toward the bed.

"Whoa, wait. I don't have protection," he whispered against her neck. "I didn't even think about it with you kissing me like that. I want you, Flo. I just never expected this."

Flo glanced at the jacket she had tossed away, cursing herself for not being prepared either, and then she saw foil from a strip of condoms sticking out from the breast pocket.

"What about those?"

Nate glanced over his shoulder and then shook his head. "Kyle. This is his tuxedo."

"I don't think he'll mind." Flo grinned.

"I don't care if he does. I wasn't going to ever ask him. I'm just going to take what I want." He scooped her up in his arms and carried her to the bed, laying her down and moving over her. She ran her hands over his partly exposed chest.

He sat up and whipped off his shirt. All that was between them now was his trousers and her underwear. Just scraps of fabric.

"There's something else I need to tell you," Flo whispered as he nibbled on her neck. "I'm a virgin."

He froze and she was worried that her virginity would be the deal-breaker. It wouldn't be the iffy future because of the donated kidney, it would be because he didn't want to deflower a thirty-something virgin.

"How can that be?" he asked in disbelief.

She blushed, embarrassed to tell him this, but she hadn't wanted to spring it on him. He'd have found out soon enough. "Do you want to leave?"

"No, I just don't understand how someone as beautiful and sexy as you still is a virgin."

"It takes a lot for me to trust anyone with my past. I'm glad I shared it with you and that I waited."

He kissed her and she was lost, melting into him. "I'll be gentle."

Flo sighed and he moved off the bed. She watched him undress, her pulse racing as she drank in the sight of him naked. This was finally going to happen and she was more than ready.

Nate came back to her and slipped off her underwear before holding her tight against him. She trembled and he kissed her.

"Don't be nervous."

"I'm not."

He stroked her cheek and kissed her again, his hand trailing down over her abdomen and then lower. Touching her intimately. Her body thrummed with desire. She arched her body against his fingers, craving more. Wanting him. Nate moved his hand, pinning her to the bed as he shifted his weight.

"Do you want me, Flo?" he asked some time later, his voice hoarse.

"I do."

Their gazes locked as he entered her. She winced, but the pain was brief compared to all the procedures she'd gone through in her life.

"I'm sorry," he whispered.

"I'm not." She kissed him and he began to move gently. Slowly. He was taking his time. She wrapped her arms around him to hold him close as he made love to her. He kissed her again and then trailed his kisses down her neck to her collar bone. It made her body arch and she wanted more of him. She wanted him deeper and she wrapped her legs around his waist, begging him to stay close.

Her body felt alive. She had never thought a feeling like this would be possible. She had never thought that she would ever get to experience it. She'd hoped one day to, but the one man she had truly cared about had run from her when he'd found out about her past, and she wasn't the type of girl to hand over her first time to a random stranger.

Even though her relationship with Nate was not real and he'd leave once Kyle was gone, she was glad to have her first time with him. She trusted him.

Maybe love?

She shook that thought away. There was no room in her life for love.

There was just this moment.

She wanted to savor it. He quickened his pace and she came, crying out as the heady pleasure flooded through her veins. Nate soon followed and then rolled away, pulling her with him.

Flo rested her head against his chest, listening to his heart race.

Savoring her stolen moments.

CHAPTER ELEVEN

NATE FELL ASLEEP next to Flo. He hadn't intended to spend the night. He hadn't spent the night with anyone since Serena, and for one moment he had forgotten how *good* it felt to be with someone again. To spend the night next to someone, listening to them breathe.

Knowing that they were alive and not a ghost, haunting him.

He propped himself on one elbow to watch her sleep. A little crack of sunlight peeked through the drapes and a light warm breeze was blowing in through the sliding glass doors, but she was oblivious to all of it.

She was so beautiful with her ebony hair fanned out on the pillow, her plump lips pressed together in a pout and her delicate hands folded together on top of her chest. A strand of her silky hair curled around a pink nipple and he had to tear his gaze away from her, because he wanted her again.

It took all of his willpower not to wake her up and take her in his arms again, but he couldn't do that. He'd had a moment of weakness and that was all. There couldn't be any more. No matter how much he wanted it. Memories of being buried in her, wrapped in her arms, were still fresh in his mind. The feel of her tender, soft lips against his, her nails down his back and her legs around his waist as he'd thrust into her fired his blood more.

Flo stirred and then opened her eyes to look at him, a blush creeping into her cheeks. "Good morning."

"Good morning," he replied. "I hope I didn't wake you."

"No. You didn't. I forgot you were there for a while. I didn't know where I was at first."

He chuckled. "You've already put me from your mind, then?"

"No, I just haven't slept that well in a long time." She stretched and rolled over on her side, tucking her arms under her head. "What time is it?"

Nate glanced over at the alarm clock behind him. "Six a.m. Early."

"Well, we did skip out on the gala early." Flo laughed softly. "Yes. I'm sure we'll get an earful when we get back to the clinic."

"Right. We'll have to head there soon. Today is the big day. Eva's transplant surgery."

Flo nodded. "It is."

"How are you feeling about it?" Nate asked.

"I'm feeling good."

He nodded. Everything about Flo impressed him, but it had all made perfect sense to him when she'd told the audience why they should become organ donors, why she didn't drink and why she understood her patients so well.

And why she felt every loss, why she connected with her patients so deeply. Then it occurred to him that she had a bucket list and had made several references to fleeting time.

"This bucket list of yours," he said.

"What about this bucket list of mine?" she asked.

"Why do you have it? Is it just for fun or something serious?"

"It's serious. I spent all my childhood on the sidelines due to overprotective parents who thought I might shatter at any moment. So I started compiling a list of all the things I wanted to do when I became an adult. I haven't done much because of schooling and work, but life is short. Failure rates are high. Who knows how much longer I have left?" Flo rolled over and began to pull on her clothes.

Who knows how much longer I have left?

"Flo, you realize that as you had your transplant at fourteen, you know you're doing quite well. You've come so far."

"I know," she said offhandedly as she put her long hair back in a ponytail. "Still, I do want to *live* while I have the chance."

"What else is on this bucket list? I know driving was on there."

She glanced over her shoulder at him. "You seriously want to know?"

"Sure."

"Well, you know about the mountain climbing, like Everest or walking the Annapurna trail. I would like to ride a motorcycle through Africa. Or swim with sharks."

"Hold up, you were terrified of sharks when we were surfing."

She chuckled. "I know, but this would be in a cage."

Nate sat there listening to her talk about all these dangerous things she wanted to do. Things that he'd done himself, so he knew for a fact how risky they were, and he couldn't figure out why she wanted to do these things. She'd been given a second chance, why would she risk throwing it all away by doing something dangerous?

"I also want to do some rock climbing and tackle El Capitan in Yosemite."

That caught his attention and caused his stomach to clench as the memory of Serena slipping out of his grasp as she'd fallen from the halfway point of El Capitan all those years ago. It made him sweat, made him sick to his stomach to think about Flo up there.

She could fall. She could die. Just like Serena had. And then what would he do? And the fact she evoked this feeling in him, these emotions scared him. Made him retreat further behind the careful walls he'd built for himself.

Walls that were there so he wouldn't get hurt again, because he never wanted to feel that kind of pain again.

El Capitan was too dangerous. Risking her life for all these foolish bucket-list ideas was too dangerous. Why did she have to do these things?

It's not your concern.

She was throwing it all away, but he couldn't tell her that because it wasn't his business. They weren't anything to each other. This whole relationship had just been an act to protect The Hollywood Hills Clinic.

Once everything was done with Kyle and Eva he'd go back to New York. That's where he belonged.

Besides, a fling with a colleague was probably on Flo's bucket list, he just didn't want to know that. It was better it was left this way.

Is it? She did give her virginity to you.

She had to get rid of it some time. He was just the one she'd chosen. He should've refused. He shouldn't have let her kiss him. He should've been stronger.

"Sounds like your bucket list is pretty sorted." He rolled out of bed and started to get dressed; he could feel Flo's gaze boring into him.

"Are you okay?" she asked.

"I'm fine. I just want to have a shower and go over some stuff before tonight." He zipped up his pants. "Maybe catch a nap. I didn't sleep much last night."

She laughed and then pulled on her dress from the night before. She had a change of clothes but she wanted to feel the fabric on her skin and to relive the memory of everything that had happened for just a little longer. "Can you help me with the back?"

"Sure." He took a deep breath, trying not to forget that she was off-limits to him. So he quickly did up the clasps that he had been more than happy to undo the night before. Once they were done up he took a step back, because he knew that if he didn't put distance between the two of them he was liable to fall back into that sweet trap again.

She turned around and touched his face. "Thank you again for last night. I'm glad it was you."

"I'm glad, too."

Are you?

"I hope you know that I don't expect anything. I don't—"

"I know," he said, cutting her off. "I appreciate it."

She didn't look convinced, but he didn't want to spend the day talking about this with her. He didn't have time for that.

What's done was done and he could move on.

Can you?

Flo walked back into the hospital. She'd gone home from the hotel, had taken a shower, a power nap and drunk a whole lot of coffee to get her up to fighting standard for Eva's big surgery this evening.

She wasn't going to let Eva down.

Flo was going to do everything in her power to make sure that this kidney stuck. That it wasn't rejected. Not that she had any power over that. Rejection happened, but she was going to do her best to get Eva to fighting standard, as well.

As she walked to her office she caught sight of Nate, standing at a nursing station. He was typing something into one of the tablets and she could see a couple of the nurses eyeing him with admiration.

She couldn't blame them.

Just looking at him made her weak in the knees. Even more so now that she knew what was under those scrubs. She knew what he felt like and the memory of his lips on her skin, his body beneath her thighs, his hands in her hair made her blood heat and made her recall the pleasure he had made her feel.

Pleasure that she'd never thought was possible.

Her body responded to just the mere thought of him.

It scared her.

She was glad that Nate had been her first time. It's what she'd wanted and she kept telling herself that it was just a fling, nothing more. Yet the more she said it, the more ridiculous it sounded to her; the more she realized that being with him had probably been a huge mistake for her heart.

It was more than just a fling to her and that was terrifying.

Flo shook the little kernel of thought that there could be something more out of her head. They were just friends. Work colleagues. Both of them had always made that clear. There could never be any more.

If she tried to make it more than it was she'd get hurt. Hadn't she learned already that there was no room in her life for romance or any kind of emotional attachment beyond her immediate family?

Nate was all fine and dandy now with her kidney transplant, but he knew the facts. He knew that her time was precarious. Eventually he'd leave for someone more stable.

So, no, there couldn't ever be any more between them.

Even if she secretly wished there could be.

She tore her gaze away from him and tried to make it to her office without being seen by anyone. She needed a few moments alone to regroup and prepare for Eva's surgery. There was a lot riding on it.

This was the first transplant surgery arranged between The Hollywood Hills Clinic and the Bright Hope Clinic. She knew there was some stuff from the past between the Rothsbergs and Mila Brightman, something about a wedding—Flo really didn't know. All she knew was she had to be on her top game.

This surgery meant a lot and the world would be watching.

She was well aware that the news of this surgery had reached far beyond Los Angeles, because the email from her father that morning and the countless text messages from her mother had let her know exactly how far the news had spread.

They weren't concerned about the surgery and whether or not she could pull it off. They wanted to know who Nate was and why she hadn't told them about her relationship with him. How could she lie to her parents? She'd never lied to them before. There was nothing to say about the relationship between her and Nate because there was nothing there.

Really?

There was something there, at least on her end, but she refused to admit it. She refused to give in to her emotions, because there was no place for them.

There was no place for love.

And putting a name to the emotions was out of the question.

She got to her office and sat down. The light on her phone was flashing and she had no doubt some of those messages had to be from her parents. The rest would be from various newspapers and magazines, wanting updates on Kyle's condition and her relationship with Nate. Flo had no time to deal with any of that.

She didn't want to deal with that.

Not today.

"I was wondering what time you were going to come in," Nate said as he barged into the office.

"I had a nap. You said I should nap."

"So I did." He set down the tablet he'd been carrying and sat down on the couch. "Are you ready for tonight?"

She nodded. "I think so. You?"

"I am. I did a few laps in the pool this morning after I got back to my place. I needed to take the edge off. I've done kidney surgeries countless times, but today... I don't know what it is but I feel a bit on edge about it. Like I'm under pressure."

"Yeah, I understand. I'm feeling the same way." Flo leaned back in her chair. "There's a lot riding on this."

Nate nodded. "Look, about last night..."

She shook her head. "I don't want to talk about last night. Not right now. I just want to keep my focus on Eva."

"Fair enough. Nothing from UNOS?"

"You mean about Kyle? No, nothing." Flo scrubbed her hand over her face. "Have you been to see him?"

"I have his recent labs here." Nate handed her the tablet. "It's not good."

Flo glanced at the vitals and the labs from first thing this morning to only an hour ago. Kyle's condition was deteriorating rapidly.

Blast.

"He needs organs."

Nate nodded. "He needed them yesterday. If it continues to climb this way he's going to go into multi-system organ failure and then there's nothing we can do. He'll die."

"Yeah, and the world will say we're responsible." Flo groaned. "What're we going to do?"

"There's nothing we can do. We just have to wait. It's the hardest part. We'll continue to draw blood, monitor his situation and just hope for the best."

"Have faith?" she asked.

"Yeah, that, too." He smiled at her. It was a kind and tender smile. It made her swoon. There were so many things she adored about him.

Stop thinking like that. Get a grip on yourself.

"It's hard to have faith. It's hard to sit here and wait for someone else to die so that our patient can go on living." It was the one thing she hated about the job.

"I know." There was a change in Nate's demeanor, as if he'd pulled away. He could barely look her in the eye. She didn't like that.

At least he's not pitying you, like everyone else.

"How are we going to attack this surgery? We've talked about our plan before, but never really firmed up details."

Nate nodded. "I think that I should retrieve it and you should reattach it."

"Have them in the same OR?" Flo asked. "We have an OR that is large enough and has been put on hold for me indefinitely."

"I think that's wise. Less travel time for the kidney. Less chance of contamination, and it minimizes the cold ischemic time or for something else to happen. This kidney is Eva's best shot."

Flo smiled. "Is it? And you're the one who wanted to wait for a deceased donor kidney."

"I know. You were right."

She grinned and leaned back. "Say it again."

Nate laughed and rolled his eyes. "You. Were. Right."

"I know."

"So does that plan work for you?" Nate asked.

"Yes. I'll let the surgical team know." Flo stood up. "For what it's worth, I'm glad you're going to be with me tonight. It's going to make the surgery so much easier having such a skilled transplant surgeon working with me."

"My pleasure," Nate said quietly.

She nodded and left her office quickly. If she stayed she might say a few other things that she wanted to say. Things that she wasn't sure she wanted to even admit to herself.

Like the fact that she was very close to falling in love with Nate.

Something she'd promised herself she wouldn't do when she'd slept with him, but that was easier said than done.

CHAPTER TWELVE

FLO STOOD AT the door to Eva's suite. The nurses were milling about, taking care of last-minute preparations on Eva. Eva looked absolutely terrified. Flo knew exactly how she was feeling and seeing the terror on Eva's face brought it all back afresh to her. At The Hollywood Hills Clinic she did a lot of transplant surgery and consultation on transplants. She'd even done a lot of kidney transplants with both deceased donors and living donors. But they had all been adults.

She hadn't worked on a child since her days as a resident and even then she hadn't done a kidney transplant on a child ever as a lead surgeon and not an assist. There were a few technical differences. Eva was twelve so it would be similar to doing the procedure on an adult, but, like Flo, Eva had been a preemie. Her vessels could be smaller, which meant Flo would have to try a different approach. She wouldn't know until she got in there and that was the maddening thing about surgery and the practice of medicine.

At least it was maddening for her.

Skill-wise, the surgery was the same. Ms. Martinez's kidney would be of adult size and the donor kidney would be placed in the same location as Flo's had been, the cradle of the pelvis. Technically, everything would go easily. Of that Flo had no doubt, but emotionally this was harder than she had ever imagined.

You need to talk to her.

Flo took a deep breath and headed toward Eva. The nurses finished up and left the room, and Flo took a seat on the edge of the child's bed.

"It's okay to be scared," she said.

Eva looked at her. "It is?"

"Of course, but I will tell you it will be okay. You'll feel better."

Eva shrugged. "How do you know it will be okay?"

Flo lifted up her scrub shirt. "See this scar?"

"Yeah."

"When I was fourteen I was the one in a hospital bed, waiting for a kidney."

Eva's eyes widened. "You?"

Flo nodded. "Me. Only my mom and dad weren't a match. I had to wait a long time. I almost didn't make it while I waited for someone special to give me a second chance. You're very lucky. Your mom was a match."

"I don't want my mom to get hurt."

Flo squeezed her hand. "She'll hurt for a while. You will, too, but it would hurt your mom far worse if she didn't do this and something happened to you."

Tears rolled down Eva's face and Flo hugged her. "It will be okay. You'll both heal and this will be behind you. Then I want you to do something for me."

"What?" Eva asked, wiping her eyes.

"I want you to live. Make a difference."

She smiled. "How?"

Flo shrugged. "That's up to you. I became a surgeon who helps people like us. Your future is up to you now, because you *have* a future, thanks to your mom."

"Dr. Chiu, we're ready to take Eva down now," a porter said from the door.

Flo nodded and then stood. "I'll see you in a bit and I'll see you on the other side. Just think, no more dialysis. You'll be able to play sports within reason, learn to drive. Go to dances."

Eva smiled. "That's a good thing."

Flo chuckled and walked out of the room and headed toward the OR floor. There were always risks associated with organ transplants. Always. The graft could fail, Eva's body could reject her mother's organ, but she had a good feeling about this surgery.

The allograft survival rate was high for those who got a living kidney compared to people like her who had received their kidney from a deceased patient. She also completely trusted Nate, who was doing the retrieval.

Before she had really got to know him, when he'd first arrived, she had looked him up. Read his research papers and discovered that he was one of the surgeons who could do a live donor kidney retrieval laparoscopically. Flo knew what a technical challenge it was to do a retrieval that way, but Ms. Martinez's recovery time would be exponentially cut in half.

She'd only be in the hospital two to four days compared to the six to eight weeks if it was done via laparotomy. They hadn't even been sure that they could do it laparoscopically on Ms. Martinez until after Nate examined her and found her health in good order. She was the perfect candidate.

The large OR was big enough to allow Flo to work on Eva and allow Nate and the laparoscopic equipment to be on the other side of the room.

She headed into the scrub room and ran into Nate, who was scrubbing up. He glanced at her. "How is Eva doing?"

"She's scared. Unsurprisingly." Flo stepped on the foot pedal to start the water. "I told her it would be okay."

"Normally I wouldn't tell a patient that, given all the variables, but I have a good feeling about this one." Nate smiled at her. "Ms. Martinez is very determined."

Flo nodded. "You can't get in the way of a mama bear protecting her cub."

"Is that what it is?"

"Sure, of course." Flo chuckled. "My mom was a force to be reckoned with in the children's hospital where I had my surgery done."

"I can see that. You're sometimes a force to be reckoned with." Nate shook water off his hands and grabbed a paper towel. "I think this will be okay. I'm very skilled."

"I know you are," she teased, causing him to laugh.

"I meant at laparoscopic surgery."

"I know." Flo glanced through the window into the OR. She could see Ms. Martinez on the surgical table, mouthing words with her eyes closed. It took Flo a fraction of a second to realize she was praying.

"I'll see you in there," Nate said, disappearing through the sliding door into the OR.

Flo finished her scrubbing and sent out her own silent prayer. She needed this to work. She'd promised Eva. As she finished scrubbing, Eva was wheeled in to where she got to reach out and hold her mother's hand, just briefly, before being taken to the opposite side of the OR.

She herself walked into the OR, where a nurse helped her into a gown and gloved her. Flo headed over to Ms. Martinez, who was crying.

"Ms. Martinez, it's Flo."

Ms. Martinez glanced up at her. "I'm sorry for crying."

"Don't be sorry. Everything will be okay. It will be

fine. I'll take good care of Eva and Nate will take good care of you. She'll come through like I did."

"You?"

Flo nodded. "Me, and I was only two years older than Eva at the time."

Ms. Martinez nodded and Flo walked toward Eva. The scrub team was going over the safety precautions and Ms. Martinez was put under general anesthetic. Flo glanced back once to watch Nate as he went into action.

That part was in his hands now. He'd retrieve the kidney and Flo had to prepare Eva so that when the kidney was brought across the room, she could start implanting it.

"Flo?" Eva said questioningly through the oxygen mask.

"I'm here, Eva. Can you count back for me? It's time to sleep."

Eva nodded and started to drift.

Flo turned to the nurse. "Insert a catheter and then a bag of methylene blue and Ancef. I want to make sure I can see her bladder and not hit the peritoneum or bowel."

"Yes, Dr. Chiu."

Flo took a deep breath and waited for the dye and the catheter. All she could think about was the time she had been on the table in Eva's place. Eva had a better shot than she herself ever had.

You're here, though. You beat the odds.

Once she had successful confirmation that everything was a go, she got ready to work. All that mattered was making sure that Eva had the best shot at success. When that press conference took place tomorrow afternoon, she wanted to walk in there and tell them that the first transplant surgery between The Hollywood Hills Clinic and the Bright Hope Clinic had been a complete success and that mother and daughter would both make a complete recovery.

That was what Flo focused on as she worked and prepared the area.

As she readied the field where she would connect the kidney she heard, "Walking with the kidney."

She glanced up to see a surgical resident from the Bright Hope Clinic walking toward her with the kidney in a metal bowl full of ice. A perfect, healthy kidney, which had been taken from mother and was about to be implanted into the daughter.

Ms. Martinez had given Eva life. Twice.

It was a beautiful thing. It was a bit of joy.

The resident who was assisting her took the bowl from the other resident and prepped the kidney with solution, getting it ready for Flo to implant it in the intraperitoneum as Eva's external iliac vessels were too small. A slight change of plan, but one that Flo could easily handle.

"Walking with the kidney," her resident called as she carefully scooped up the kidney and handed it to Flo.

Flo cradled the kidney in her hand, marveling at it. Such an important organ. Just as important as any other organ and the most wonderful gift that she herself had been given. In time Eva would understand too what a gift she'd received.

A second chance at life.

Flo placed the kidney into the cavity and began the anastomosis. Eva's arteries and veins were delicate and her mother's donated kidney a little large, but she'd get it to work. Nate came over and stood on the other side.

"Can I assist you, Dr. Chiu?"

"Is Ms. Martinez okay?"

"She's on her way to Recovery. Everything is good and she came through beautifully."

Thank God.

"You can help," Flo said. "Her vessels are small and anatomizing to the aorta is a bit tricky. I was hoping she'd have larger vessels, being twelve, but her premature birth stunted some things."

Nate leaned over. "You're doing great and almost there." He continued to offer her words of encouragement as well as check on Eva's condition.

The blue dye allowed her to see the bladder when she attached the ureter.

And when she was done the kidney pinked up and a stream of urine shot out, letting her know that the kidney was functioning.

"Excellent job, Dr. Chiu!" Nate exclaimed as the surgical team applauded.

Tears stung Flo's eyes and she laughed when she saw that stream of urine. "Let's close her up."

Nate stepped in and they closed her up, making sure everything was where it was supposed to be. A pressure dressing was placed on the wound then Eva was rolled into the post-anesthesia recovery unit, where she would be extubated from her general anesthesia.

When that stream of urine had flowed, Flo had wanted to shout for joy, because the surgery had been a success so far, but there was still recovery and monitoring of Eva in the ICU to make sure that she didn't reject the organ or have stenosis or a clot. There were still so many risk factors for Eva, but so far she'd taken a step in the right direction.

There was still a long road to go, which was why Flo didn't want to give an update on Eva until tomorrow afternoon.

Right now she was exhausted.

She peeled off her surgical gown and mask, stuffing them into the appropriate receptacles, before scrubbing out.

Nate was beside her again.

"Good work, Dr. King," Flo said.

"Removing a donor kidney is easy—you had the hard job."

"Your job was just as technically challenging, Nate. Don't sell yourself short."

He smiled at her and toweled off. "How should we celebrate?"

"Celebrate?"

"We have to celebrate a bit."

"How about a pizza at my place? Usually I wouldn't have someone over to my place, but I'm wiped out and don't have the energy to bike home."

Nate laughed. "So that's why you're inviting me over. Sure. We can do that."

"Thank you." Flo dried her hands. "I'm going to check on them post-op and give my orders. Then pizza."

He nodded. "I'll meet you out front in an hour."

Nate watched Flo leave the scrub room.

What are you doing?

He really didn't know. After what had happened between the two of them last night and his absolute loss of control, he'd promised himself that would never happen again. For one moment, being with her now, he'd forgotten that he didn't do those kinds of things any more. They weren't a real couple.

He swore he wouldn't do things like surfing or racing or one-night stands again.

Nate strode toward the exit, mad at himself for letting

Flo in. It had been so easy for her to get past his defenses, under his armor. He couldn't let that happen tonight.

He'd celebrate with her because what they had just done together, saving Eva's life and completing a successful kidney transplant, was something worth celebrating. He could celebrate with Flo as her friend, because that's all it could be.

He had to remember to keep his distance after this.

He had to remind himself why he was here and that being in California was only temporary. His life was waiting for him in New York.

A lonely life.

A lonely life it may be, but it was what he deserved. He'd lived too recklessly as a young man and it had cost a life. Loneliness was the penance he gladly paid.

Or at least it had used to be.

CHAPTER THIRTEEN

"Did you check on Ms. Martinez?" Flo asked as she rummaged around in her fridge.

"I did," Nate said as he took a seat at her island. Flo's apartment was small and her tiny table was covered with an assortment of medical journals and papers. At least the piles were neat. She seemed to thrive on orderly chaos, if that was possible. So they were having their pizza celebration dinner at her kitchen counter. Which was fine.

If he didn't get too comfortable he wouldn't have the impetus to stay or linger.

"How was she?" Flo asked.

"Relieved." Nate smiled to himself as he recalled telling Ms. Martinez how well the surgery had gone. How her daughter was strong and stable in the pediatric ICU and being monitored, and that so far there wasn't any sign of rejection.

The joy on her face made his job worthwhile.

Though both he and Flo had their phones out in front of them. Ready to jump at a moment's notice if a call came from the hospital that something was up with Eva or Ms. Martinez. Or if there were organs for Kyle again, because Kyle was not doing well.

His time was running out and that weighed heavily on Nate.

He'd been Kyle's physician for a long time and watching Kyle slowly die was taking its toll on him. He wanted so much for organs to be found, but his hopes were waning fast. He was losing patience. He wanted organs for Kyle so Kyle wouldn't die and so he could go home to New York. There were too many ghosts in California for his liking.

Los Angeles brought up too many bad memories. He also had to get away from Flo. Distance would be the best for them.

"How about grape soda? It's not wine, but I can't have wine."

"Sure," Nate said. "You know that it's okay for you to have alcohol every once in a while."

Flo shrugged. "I know. Two units a day, but really I don't want to risk it. Alcohol raises your blood pressure and I want to keep my kidneys for a long time."

She set down a tumbler and poured some grape soda into it.

"I feel like I'm ten years old during summer vacation." He took a sip and winced. "Just as I remember."

"It's not that bad." Flo then pulled a piece of paper out of her pocket and set it down in front of Nate.

"What's this?"

"It's part of my bucket list. It's what I want to do to celebrate Eva's successful surgery. I told her that she needed to go on living when she recovered."

A sense of dread filled Nate as he unfolded the paper and found himself staring at a picture of El Capitan in Yosemite. The sheer rock wall brought back the moment, which had been over a decade ago, flooding back to him, like it was fresh and new all over again.

"Hold on, Serena. Please hold on."

"I can't. I can't."

Nate crumpled the picture in his fist, trying to drown out the screams in his head.

"What're you doing?" Flo asked shocked.

"This is a bad idea," Nate said.

"Why?"

"El Capitan is the tallest vertical face. It's three thousand feet high from base to summit. Do you know how dangerous it is to climb?"

"I'm aware of how tall it is, but a lot of people climb it."

"Skilled climbers, and even then they die!" he shouted at her. Didn't she get it? She'd been given a second chance at life, yet she kept wanting to do these risky and strange things. Why was she trying to end her life? She'd been given a second chance when Serena hadn't. Flo was reckless.

You were reckless once, too.

"What has gotten into you? Why are you so angry?"

"Why are you throwing away your life?"

She took a step back from him, confused. "Throwing my life away?"

"Yes. You've been given a second chance so why are you risking your life, doing these dangerous things? Why do you even need a bucket list?"

"I need a bucket list because I don't know how much time I have left," she snapped.

Now it was his turn to be confused. "You said that before. What're you talking about? You had a kidney donation. Is your kidney failing?"

"No, but you know the failure rates. How long can a deceased organ really last? It may not last a lifetime. I've already surpassed fifteen years. I don't have many left."

"Do you hear yourself? You've passed fifteen years and aren't in renal failure. Why are you risking your health, wanting to do dangerous, stupid things? You avoid alcohol and I would say that's a lot safer than climbing El Capitan. You're throwing your life away."

It was like a slap to the face. She'd thought he would understand her passion to try new things. She'd told him how she'd spent her life on the sidelines, watching and never able to participate. Flo had thought he understood her.

She'd thought that he didn't pity her, but apparently she'd been wrong, because he was treating her like a fragile thing. Like she was about to shatter at any moment if she continued to try and live her life.

"I'm not throwing away my life. I'm living it until I can't any more."

"You still have years left, but if you continue down this trajectory, you won't. You'll get yourself killed and what kind of thanks would that be to your organ donor?"

He was stifling her. Just like her parents always tried to do. This was why love and romance wasn't for her. Fall in love and suddenly that other person tried to control your life. "How dare you? You don't know me."

"Don't I?" Nate rubbed his face.

"No. You don't. I'm making the most of my time. I'm not being ungrateful by putting my life at risk. I'm living my life to the fullest."

"No, you're not, because you don't understand the consequences."

"And you do?" Flo asked.

"I do." His expression changed from one of anger to one of sadness.

"I'm sorry you lost a friend while they waited on the list, but this isn't the same thing."

"Of course it is. They wouldn't have acted so recklessly."

"I'm not reckless. And what would you know about that? You're so rigid and guarded. You said you used to climb mountains, so why don't you any more? What happened?"

Nate sighed. "Before I entered medical school I lived like you. I took risks. In fact, the riskier the better as far as I was concerned, and my girlfriend Serena lived the same way. We were adrenaline junkies. We were also experienced rock climbers. We were always at the gym, practicing rappelling. We knew what we were doing until we didn't.

"Then, during a climb, halfway up El Capitan, Serena's rope slipped, the carabiner failed and she fell. She died in the hospital with multiple injuries, needing organs, but there were none to be had and she was far down the list because of her trauma. It was my fault she died. I don't remember if I checked everything as thoroughly as I should've. That's why doing these risky, foolish things is a waste, Flo. You're risking your life for a second of adrenaline. A minute of thrill. That's it. Life is not worth that."

Flo was saddened to hear his admission. He'd been carrying around guilt for so long that it had eaten away at him. She'd thought he was pitying her, trying to hold her back, like her parents did, because he didn't think she could physically do it, but it was something more.

He was afraid for her.

He was angry at her.

Nate claimed that she was wasting her life by doing such risky things, as if her time was up. And maybe he was right, but he was wasting his own life, letting the ghosts of the past hold him back. He was hiding behind walls of guilt and pain.

It was tragic Serena had died and that he blamed himself, but he was throwing away his own life by not living. Two people had died on that mountain, Serena and Nate.

"You have lots of time left, Flo. Don't risk that time by doing something stupid," Nate snapped.

"You're one to talk."

"What's that supposed to mean?"

"It means at least I'm out there, trying to live."

He snorted. "That's not living."

"And hiding behind guilt, letting guilt keep you back from ever having happiness again, is living? Maybe you're the one who needs to start living again. Maybe you need to take some risks."

Nate didn't say anything else to her. He just turned on his heel and left her apartment. The door slammed behind him.

Flo sighed. It had hurt, saying those things to him. She hadn't wanted to, but he'd said some hurtful things to her.

Only he's right.

She bent down and picked up the crumpled picture of El Capitan. Did she really want to do this?

No. Not really. She'd picked it because it had been the most advanced thing she could think of. Nate did have a point. Why was she so adamant on doing stuff she wasn't capable of doing? Maybe after some training she could tackle El Capitan.

Maybe Nate was right about it all.

Had she been so bent on proving to the world about what she could do, because for so long everyone she cared about had said she couldn't, that she was really risking this precious gift she'd been given? And in that pursuit she'd pushed away everyone, including the man she was in love with.

The realization hit her hard because even though she didn't want to fall in love with Nate, she was in love with him. And she had been so scared about him pitying her or keeping her from doing what she wanted that she'd pushed him away.

The tears began to flow down her face and there was no stopping them.

All these years she'd thought she'd been living her life, but she really hadn't been.

Flo didn't sleep well that night so instead she headed back over to the hospital and spent the night in the ICU next to Eva, watching her urine output and monitoring her vitals. There was no sign of Nate and it was better that way.

After what had happened between the two of them, Flo doubted she'd ever see him again outside work and the facade they had to put on. Even then, they seemed to have convinced the press a while ago that they were indeed dating, because the furor had died down.

There was no story to tell.

No scandal.

Everyone was just waiting for organs for Kyle Francis.

All she had to do was get through the press conference about Eva and, thankfully, she could present good news. She just hoped that she could hold it all together in front of Nate. Her heart was racing as she entered the press room. Freya and Mila were waiting for her and a smattering of press was assembled.

Flo shook their hands and smiled, silently letting the two of them know that the surgery had been a success. That she was here to deliver good news rather than bad. She glanced around, but Nate was nowhere to be seen.

And she was a bit disappointed.

What did you expect?

Flo took the podium and the din of chatter died down. "Thank you all for coming here today. Last night at approximately nineteen hundred hours Eva Martinez and her mother were taken to the OR at The Hollywood Hills Clinic where a successful live donor transplant took place. Ms. Martinez went through a laparoscopic left kidney retrieval performed by Dr. King and came through her donation with flying colors. Her surgery was minimal compared to an open dissection method."

As she said his name the door opened and he slid in, standing at the back. His face was unreadable as he leaned against the wall with his arms crossed.

Ignore him.

"I performed the anastomosis of Eva Martinez's kidney with implantation onto the aorta and IVC, intra-peritoneal."

"Can you explain why you chose that method over using the external iliac vessels?"

"I approached it this way because Eva's vessels were too small given her age," Flo said. "Pediatric external iliac vessels can be too small sometimes."

The reporter nodded and jotted down notes.

"Eva is doing well in the ICU and is expected to a make a full recovery."

There was applause and that's when Nate began to make his way to the front. Her heart sank. She prayed it wasn't Eva.

"I'm sorry for interrupting," Nate said. "Dr. Chiu, can I speak with you a moment?"

Flo stepped away from the microphone and Nate leaned over, whispering in her ear, "There are organs for Kyle across town."

Then, before she could say anything further, he moved away from her, like he couldn't stand to be near her, and left the press room. Everyone was watching her, the room silent.

"I'm afraid I have to leave. Thank you, everyone." Flo

quickly turned on her heel and ran out of the press room, ignoring the rapid-fire questions of people asking if this was about Kyle. She'd let Freya and Mila deal with that mess. They were better at it.

Right now she had an important job to do.

Kyle didn't have much time left. He needed those organs.

Please, God. Let them be viable this time.

And since it was across town she'd get there in time to perform the examination of those organs herself this time.

Nate was waiting outside the press room.

"I'll prep Kyle. You go and get the organs," he said quickly. Then he handed her her cell phone. "You forgot this in your office. You almost missed the UNOS call."

"Sorry. Okay, and thanks."

He nodded, but he wouldn't look at her. "Call me when you have the organs. There's an ambulance waiting for you."

Before she had a chance to say anything else he turned his back on her and walked away, off to prep Kyle. Flo headed to where the ambulance was waiting for her. They had the equipment she needed and once she was in the back of the ambulance the paramedic shut the door and the siren blared. They took off across Los Angeles.

Flo's heart hurt, but, really, what had she expected?

She'd ruined her chances with Nate. After Kyle's surgery, he'd return to New York and she very much doubted she'd see him again.

It nearly killed Nate to see Flo. He'd planned to keep his distance from her today, but then he'd got the message from UNOS and had had to face her.

At least he had the excitement of telling Kyle about the organs to distract him.

It killed him to watch Kyle suffer. But now he had a real chance.

Kyle was conscious, but barely, as Nate walked into his room.

"Hey, Doc," Kyle whispered.

"Good news. We've found organs again. Dr. Chiu is on her way to retrieve them. This time they're not so far. Only across town. We need to get you prepped and into the OR."

Kyle smiled weakly. "That's great, but forgive me for not holding my breath. Also because I can't really. Bad lungs."

Nate chuckled. "Yes. Please, don't."

"So, you never did tell me how the tuxedo worked out."

"Didn't I?" Nate said, trying to ignore Kyle's questions. He didn't want to talk about Flo here. It was too raw.

"No. You didn't. Come on, what happened?"

"We went to the gala and raised money."

Kyle rolled his eyes. "Come on. There's been sexual tension between you two from day one. You're telling me nothing happened?"

Nate shook his head. "Really not going to talk about this with you."

Kyle grinned. "I knew it. How was it?"

"We have to draw some more blood from you before you go into the OR. I have your blood type ready and standing by for surgery."

"Come on," Kyle said. "Why don't you want to talk about your relationship with Dr. Chiu?"

"Because there is no relationship. It was a ruse. I kissed her accidentally on the rooftop once and then had to pretend I was in a relationship with her, but really there's nothing there."

Kyle's eyes narrowed. "You're such a bad liar, Doc. You care for her."

He's right.

Actually, it was more than caring for her. Nate loved Flo. He loved how strong she was. Even though she was a bit pessimistic about her own donor kidney, she still was out there, trying to live, and what had he been doing with his time? Hiding away behind guilt.

"I don't."

"I don't know why you're not admitting it when it's..." Kyle trailed off, his eyes rolling into the back of his head as he collapsed.

"Kyle?" Nate tore off his white lab coat. "Kyle?"

The monitors went nuts and Kyle flatlined.

"No, Kyle! No." Nate lunged forward and hit the code button. He lowered Kyle's bed and began CPR compressions. He couldn't shock the LVAD with an AED. As he fired off instructions for medicines, he continued his compressions.

Oh, God. Oh, God.

Kyle wasn't going to survive his own transplant surgery. No, he couldn't let his friend, his patient die. He just couldn't.

Come on. Come on.

The monitor picked up a heart rate, but every time Nate stopped compressions, Kyle crashed again.

Dammit.

His phone began to ring and a nurse picked it up.

"Dr. King, it's Dr. Chiu. She's got Mr. Francis's organs and they're viable. She said to get him into the OR."

Nate cursed under his breath and jumped onto Kyle's bed, not stopping his compressions. "Get us to the OR, stat."

The team moved quickly and Nate continued his chest

compressions on Kyle as they rolled them out of his suite and to the OR.

Nate hoped that Flo would get to them on time.

CHAPTER FOURTEEN

FLO HAD HEARD on the way back to The Hollywood Hills Clinic that Kyle had crashed. She moved as quickly as she could, yelling at people to get out of her way as she raced to the OR. When she got to there she learned that they had Kyle stabilized and Nate was performing his cardiectomy.

She scrubbed and then entered the OR. One of her younger surgeons was taking the organs and readying them for transplantation. A nurse helped Flo into her gown and she was gloved. She approached the surgical table and could see that Nate was about to remove the LVAD.

"The organs look good?" Nate asked, not looking up.

"They did. They're viable."

He nodded. "I will have the heart removed and then we can place it and work on the lungs. It will be a long haul."

"I know," Flo whispered. "Look, about—"

"I don't want to talk about it. Let's focus on Kyle, shall we?"

"Of course." Flo took her place as assist to Nate and she watched him work with bittersweet sadness, knowing that soon he would be going back to New York and she wouldn't see him again.

Even though she had resisted the idea of them pretending to be a couple to protect The Hollywood Hills Clinic, these last weeks had been the best time of her life. She'd had that bucket list for so long, but she had never really done anything about it.

Until she'd met Nate.

Not that he'd done anything risky with her, but he didn't treat her like she couldn't do things. He encouraged her, he treated her like she wasn't going to shatter at any moment, like her parents had always done.

She'd never minded being by herself. It was easier than risking her heart, as she had learned earlier on, but now that she'd had a taste of being with someone she cared about, someone she loved, she was going to miss Nate.

She was going to be lonely for a long time.

Focus.

Flo returned to the task at hand. They removed the left ventricular assist device and then went about removing Kyle's damaged heart. He was put on bypass and then they removed the lungs. The donor organs, which were in the icebox on a heart-lung machine, were brought forward. Flo took on the lungs while Nate worked on the heart.

No words were needed as they worked seamlessly together. It was like they'd been doing this kind of surgery together for years. Kyle lost a lot of blood, but blood was ready on standby for transfusion.

It was a grueling eight hours, but Flo didn't feel it. Adrenaline fueled her and when breaks were needed she took a shot of espresso, which was kept just outside the OR. Two transplant surgeries in a row and she was feeling exhausted.

"Remove the clamps," Nate said. "Let's take him off bypass."

Clamps were removed and the bypass machine was

shut down. Nate glanced at her and Flo nodded and sent up a silent prayer.

Come on.

As the machines started, Kyle's new donor heart pinked up and began to beat. His lungs moved as he took breaths. There was clapping and Flo laughed out loud.

Nate was grinning behind his surgical mask—she could tell by the way his eyes were crinkling. "Let's close him up, Dr. Chiu."

"Indeed, Dr. King."

They finished closing up Kyle, inserted drains and tubes and had him off to the post-anesthesia recovery unit. Later, if there were no problems, he would be moved up to the intensive care unit. Flo didn't plan on leaving the hospital at all. She was going to monitor Kyle all night. She peeled off her gown and disposed of it before scrubbing.

"I'll stay with Kyle tonight," Nate said. "He's my patient after all."

"Are you sure?" Flo asked. "I don't mind staying with him."

"He's not your patient. He's mine. I want to monitor him and when he's strong enough we'll take him back to New York. That's what he wants. He wants to go back to New York to recover. His parents are there."

Flo nodded and finished scrubbing. "We've managed to keep things quiet but we should speak to Freya and Kyle's people about giving a press conference about the surgery."

"You're not going to be there?"

"No."

Nate sighed. "For what it's worth, I'm glad you were in there with me."

Tears suddenly and unexpectedly stung Flo's eyes, but she wouldn't let them fall. "Me, too."

Nate left her alone and she leaned over the sink of the scrub room, letting the tears fall. Tears of regret, hurt and most of all relief.

She didn't want him to go, but she'd ruined that.

So it was best he went. Besides, how could she love a man who didn't want to be loved in return? A man who still clung to the past and punished himself for that?

The answer was that she couldn't.

Nate didn't bother changing or shaving. He just made sure his scrubs were clean. If the public wanted a press conference so badly after he had just finished an eight-hour surgery, then they could see him like this.

He walked into the press room, blinded a bit by the flashes, and took the spot at the podium.

"Thank you all for coming. As you are aware, a donor for Mr. Francis was found in a hospital about forty minutes away from The Hollywood Hills Clinic. Dr. Chiu retrieved the heart and lungs, which were found viable. After removing Mr. Francis's left ventricular assist device, Dr. Chiu and I successfully removed Mr. Francis's damaged heart and lungs and replaced them with the viable organs."

"How long did the surgery take?"

"Approximately eight hours. Mr. Francis will be in the intensive care unit for some time."

"How is his prognosis? Will he make his Broadway debut?"

"His prognosis at this moment is stable. The next forty-eight hours will give us a better picture," Nate said. "As for his Broadway debut, that will be on hold for some time. Mr. Francis's recovery will be long and he will be on anti-rejection drugs for the rest of his life."

"Where is Dr. Chiu?" someone shouted, and as Nate glanced at the man he saw Flo, in her street clothes, sneak into the back of the room. No one noticed she was there.

Seeing her made his pulse race.

Why had he had to ruin it? Why did she have to live so dangerously? The loss of control he felt around her was too much for him to bear. He had to put distance between them, even though he loved her.

"Dr. Chiu is monitoring our patient in the ICU."

"Once Mr. Francis is stable and returns to New York, what will become of your relationship with Dr. Chiu? Is this the end of the dream team?" There were a few chuckles.

"We'll see how a long-distance relationship goes." He glanced to where she was standing, but all he saw was Flo's back as she left the press room.

It killed him to hurt her.

Why did he have to hurt her?

Because you can't lose her, too.

And that was it. She was so determined to *live* her life and he wasn't. He was too scared to move forward. Too scared to lose someone he loved again that he was willing to damage his own heart.

"Now, if there are no more questions about Mr. Francis's surgery, I would really like to get back up to the ICU floor and monitor my patient." Nate excused himself, even though there was still a barrage of questions coming at him. He ran out of the press room to try and catch Flo.

There was no sign of her.

He cursed under his breath and made his way up to the ICU. When he got there, he checked on Kyle. He was still intubated, but his vitals were good. For someone who had just had a heart and lung transplant, he was doing well.

And Nate could recall the way his friend's heart had stopped under his hands. How he'd almost lost him.

"Serena, come back to me."

Only there had been no heartbeat under his hand when he'd held her. There had been nothing, just the sound of the doctor pronouncing her time of death.

When he held Flo in his arms, she was alive. She was here. Serena would want him to live on. She wouldn't have liked him living as he had been for the last decade.

Serena had been full of life.

She'd lived life to the fullest, just like Flo wanted to, and he'd never called Serena out on what she did. He'd never called her selfish for risking her life. Yet he did that with Flo.

Flo, who had fought so hard for her life.

She deserved to live it the way she wanted, and who was he to get in the way of that.

Because you don't want to lose Flo the way you lost Serena.

And that was the crux of it.

Only he didn't think he had much of a shot with Flo any more. Not after the way he'd been treating her, and he wasn't sure if he was brave enough to let Flo live the life she deserved to live. Maybe it was better for them both that he'd be leaving soon.

Flo hadn't seen Nate in three days. At first she'd thought he'd gone back to New York, but she learned from Freya that Nate was still in LA. He seemed to be working the opposite shift from her.

Which was probably for the best.

Maybe if she didn't see him again it would hurt less when he left for real.

Yet as she stood in her office, staring at the white lab coat neatly folded on the couch—his lab coat, with one of his scrub caps tucked inside—it hurt so much.

She'd thought she'd been in love before, but that wasn't true. The pain she'd felt after Johnny had left her had been nothing compared to this ache she was feeling.

I have to get out of this office.

She headed up to the ICU floor, where Kyle still was, although he would be moved back down to his suite soon if he kept doing as well as he was. Nate wasn't anywhere to be found, so Flo walked into Kyle's room.

Kyle opened his eyes and smiled, but winced just slightly. He was trying to show her that he wasn't in pain. She'd heard from one of the ICU nurses that he was trying to put on a brave face.

Flo couldn't help but chuckle. "How are you today, Mr. Francis?"

"I think I've told you to call me Kyle."

Flo nodded. "So you did. So how are you today, Kyle?"

"Sore," he whispered. "Tired. I don't think I've ever been this tired before in my life."

"Your body is healing and trying to get used to a new heart and lungs. That's a big deal."

"So I've heard." He rolled his head to one side. "How did it go, in your opinion?"

Flo sat down on the end of his bed. "It went as well as I expected. You're not showing any signs of rejection or any other post-op complications. I think that if you stay stable, tonight we can take you back to your private suite and in a month we'll have you back on that plane to New York."

"Oh," Kyle said, and he looked disappointed.

"I know you wanted to make your debut on Broadway but—"

"No, it's not that." Kyle swallowed hard. "I'm terrified, Dr. Chiu. I'm terrified at this gift I've been given."

A lump formed in Flo's throat. She understood what Kyle was feeling. There were so many times she felt that way, too. It was overwhelming.

"I understand. It's a gift that you can never send a thank-you note for. The greatest gift of all."

Kyle nodded. "That's it exactly. What if something happens...?"

"You can't live your life with the what-ifs. I lived like that for so many years." Flo sighed. "I had a kidney transplant at fourteen and I was grateful for my second chance and wanted to live, but I let my fear of life ending at any moment drive me. I felt that if I was going to die I was going to die on my own terms and not let an organ determine when that was going to happen."

"You've had a transplant?"

Flo nodded. "I know how you feel. The weight of having an organ from someone who died, it's a precious thing and I don't want you to squander it, Kyle. Live life, but live it to its proper fullest. Don't push away loved ones because of the off chance that your life might end. I mean, we never know how long our second chance at life will last, but living that second life alone...it's a life not worth living."

A tear ran down Kyle's cheek.

"That's it exactly. How long can this last?"

Flo shrugged. "I don't know. There are so many factors, but I think if you take care of yourself and the gift that you've been given, you can live a long while yet."

"Does this fear ever go away?" Kyle asked.

"No," Flo said. "It never goes away, but if you have

someone who loves you and you love them then it ma
it all worthwhile."

"Thanks, Dr. Chiu."

"Flo, remember?"

Kyle smiled. "Flo. Although I prefer to call you Florence, if you don't mind. I fell in love with a girl from Florence. She was the love of my life."

"What happened to her?"

"I let her go. The worst mistake of my life, but maybe Broadway will have to wait a little while yet. I think when I get back on my feet I'll be heading back to Italy. I want to see if I can track her down in Florence."

"I wish you all the best, Kyle." Flo got up and left Kyle's suite before she started bawling. She wished she hadn't pushed Nate away.

She wished she could have a second chance and tell Nate how she felt, that she wanted him and that she wouldn't risk her life in such a way any more.

For so long she'd lived her life saying that she wouldn't let anyone control her, tell her what she could and couldn't do, but really that didn't matter in the long run. What mattered was love.

What mattered was not pushing away those who loved you.

Life was not worth living without love.

Nate stood in the shadows and watched Flo walk away. Her head hung low and her hands were jammed in her pockets as she walked toward her office. When he'd first met her she'd held her head high and run through these halls with purpose, with drive.

This Flo was just as heartbroken as he was.

He'd come up to check on Kyle before he'd planned on finding Flo. He'd wanted to say goodbye and thank

n he'd come to Kyle's room in the ICU
ed to hear her open up to Kyle.

ame things he felt about her.

ired. He'd been living a life of guilt and fear
but that was no way to live. Flo lived a dif-
, but she lived a fear nonetheless.

just didn't let it stop her from living. Whereas
had.

He loved Flo and if she forgave him, he would spend
the rest of his life making it up to her. So instead of making a stop to see Kyle he chased after Flo.

"Dr. Chiu," he called out.

She stopped and turned around, surprised to see him.
"Dr. King? I thought you'd left for the evening."

"No, I was working in the research library. Can we
talk?"

Flo nodded and he took her arm, leading her to her office. When they were both inside he shut the door.

"I'm sorry, Flo," he whispered.

"Sorry for what?" she asked.

"Sorry for trying to stop you from living your life."

"Nate," she sighed. "You didn't."

"I did. I just… When you said you wanted to climb
El Capitan I became terrified. I couldn't lose you, Flo.
Not after losing Serena. I couldn't bear it if I lost you."

She gasped. "What?"

"I love you, Florence Chiu. I think I loved you from
the moment I first met you. I just wouldn't let myself."

"You could still lose me, though, Nate."

He shook his head. "I don't care. I know the risks,
but I don't care what will happen. I doubt anything will
happen to your donor kidney, but if something happens
I will be right by your side. I'm not going anywhere. I'm

here for the long haul. You breathed life into me again. You saved me."

"I thought I pushed you away. I've pushed away everyone. I thought I had so much to prove with that dumb bucket list, but I have nothing to prove. I let my fear rule my heart."

Nate took her in his arms and held her close. "I love you, Flo. I'm not going anywhere."

"I love you, too."

He tipped her chin and kissed her, holding her tight in his arms. She was alive. She was here and she was his.

A relationship that had started out as a facade, all because the person he used to be, the man he'd thought he'd buried a long time ago, had snuck out and kissed her. When he'd been told that he would have to pretend to be in a relationship with Flo he'd felt nervous, because he'd known that if he spent time with her he'd fall for her.

In her he saw who he used to be.

And he missed who he used to be.

With her, he could be so much more and he planned to never let her go.

Flo laid her head against his chest and sighed. "So what happens now? A long-distance relationship?"

"No, I think I'll be moving to LA. James offered me a job."

"Oh, he did?"

Nate nodded. "Also, I could really use a vacation."

"Vacation? I don't know the meaning of that word."

"I think you should learn. I think we both need a two-week vacation once Kyle is stabilized. I think we should accompany him to New York City, get him settled and my stuff dealt with, and then drive back out here. What do you think?"

"Drive across country?"

He nodded. "It was on your bucket list."

Flo groaned. "Don't even talk to me about that bucket list. It's done. It was for someone who thought she was dying. I have time."

"How about an anti-bucket list."

"What's an anti-bucket list?"

"A list of things we do while we *live.*"

Flo chuckled. "I like that idea much better. That's better than my bucket list. You're better than my bucket list."

And then she kissed him again and this time he didn't let her go.

EPILOGUE

One year later

FLO TOOK A deep breath and stood at the edge of Whistlers Mountain in Jasper National Park, staring eastward out at Canada. It wasn't Everest, but it was the highest mountain she'd ever been up, and the fact she was standing at the top, the air so cold and clear, was amazing. She could see for miles and miles. The sun was above them, but it was still morning and it was chilly. Which didn't surprise her as there was snow up at the summit of Whistlers.

Nate came up beside her and sighed, slinging his arm around her shoulder as he stood beside her on the top of the mountain, looking out at the small town of Jasper spread below their feet.

"It really is in the shape of the letter J." Flo pointed. "I didn't believe the hotel clerk when she told us."

Nate chuckled. "So untrusting."

"I trust people." She took a step away from him. "Although you have been acting mighty suspicious lately."

"I have not. See, you're totally untrusting."

"Well, you have been surprising me a lot lately. It's so unlike you." Flo grinned. "All this risk-taking."

"It's not really risk-taking, and are you telling me you don't like this surprise?"

Flo laughed and wrapped her arms around Nate. "I liked the surprise trip to Canada and I liked the surprise of climbing a mountain, even if we didn't really climb very far and it wasn't really that difficult."

"I thought taking a tram would be a nice foray into mountain climbing."

She raised an eyebrow. "The private cabin with the spring-fed hot tub is really nice, too, but it seems a bit posh. Did Kyle give you the idea?"

"He did. He knows the owners and managed to finagle a deal for us." Nate kissed the top of her head. "He wanted to do something to thank us for saving his life. He's doing a play on Broadway, but passed on the singing and dancing for now."

"That's good. I love Kyle, but he's not a singing and dancing type of actor," Flo said. "Don't tell him I said that though."

"I won't, or he'll be heartbroken. He still threatens to steal you away from me."

Flo snorted. "I'd like to see him try."

That earned her another kiss. She sighed and saw more people were taking the hour-long hike up to the summit of Whistlers. They moved off the path and headed out toward the glacier, trying to keep off to the side to enjoy their stolen moment of privacy.

Since Nate had started work at The Hollywood Hills Clinic and since their successful surgery on Kyle and the little girl Eva Martinez, people had been flocking to Los Angeles, wanting the dream team of surgeons to work on them.

Flo couldn't remember when she'd been so popular. Nate had also managed to get some more grant money for his research and he was starting a huge clinical trial at The Hollywood Hills Clinic. They hadn't had a proper vacation since they'd driven across the country together after saving Kyle's life.

They'd flown with Kyle to Manhattan and got him set up. They'd closed down Nate's practice in New York and moved him back out to Los Angeles. It had been a crazy road trip, and they'd stopped at a lot of touristy places on the two-week drive back to Los Angeles.

They had seen the Liberty Bell, had ridden on a river boat on the Mississippi. Had spent a night in the French Quarter in New Orleans, had seen Graceland and the Grand Canyon. They'd hit as many states as they could on their way back to Los Angeles. They'd even spent a night in Las Vegas before they'd meandered their way up to Seattle so that Nate could meet her parents and, of course, her *nainai*.

Surprisingly, her parents got along well with Nate. Usually both her mother and father disapproved of her dating anyone because of her health problems, but apparently that was all in the past because they wholeheartedly approved of Nate.

And Nate got along well with them.

After Seattle they'd taken a trip down to San Francisco, where Nate's parents now lived. Flo had been nervous, she'd never gone and met parents before, but they were delightful. When they'd returned to Los Angeles they'd found a bigger place near The Hollywood Hills Clinic so they could live together, and then they'd both thrown themselves into their work.

They hadn't killed each other yet.

It had been a great year.

Then last week Nate had surprised her by telling her he'd cleared her calendar. Their patients were all stable. No one was currently in dire need of organs and if they were, Nate had brought in one of his colleagues from New York to cover for them.

He'd booked two weeks off for them. They'd flown into Calgary, Alberta and then driven up to Jasper National Park, where a very private cabin had been waiting for them. The only connection they had to the outside world was a television that was hooked up to an old DVD player. The cabin had a large selection of old movies for them to watch if they got bored.

So far, Flo was not bored.

They had been hiking, they'd been to the Miette Hot Springs. They'd been white-water rafting and out to dinner. In fact, Flo was feeling a bit tired.

She was used to mountains, having grown up in Seattle, but she'd never been to the top of one. So even though she was exhausted from the supposedly relaxing, romantic vacation, she was glad to be standing at the top of this mountain, drinking in the sights around her.

Mountain climbing had been one of the things at the top of her bucket list and she knew this moment was hard for Nate, given his past. So even though they technically hadn't climbed Whistlers, other than an easy walk to the summit, the gesture was appreciated all the same.

"Thanks again for bringing me..." She trailed off when she saw that Nate had dropped to his knees. Her heart thundered in her ears. Maybe she was hallucinating. Maybe this was altitude sickness and she should get down off the mountain. "What're you doing?"

"Proposing."

She sighed in relief. "Oh, right, just like when we were surfing. Are we going to walk out on the glacier and you have to attach some kind of strap to me?"

He looked at her strangely. "No, this isn't like when we were surfing."

"What?" She began to shake. "Are you…what?"

He pulled out a box. "Flo, I'm actually proposing."

"Marriage?"

"Yes. Flo, I asked your dad's permission before we left. He was okay with it. He gave us his blessing, as did your mom. The question is, will you marry me?"

She couldn't answer him as she stared at the silvery diamond ring. She hadn't been expecting it. It was something she'd never thought twice about, because it was something she'd thought she'd never get to have, and now she was staring at it and she couldn't even find her voice.

All she could do was nod. Nate grinned and slipped the ring on her finger and then kissed her hand, followed by her lips.

"I'll take that as a yes, since you didn't fight to take the ring off."

Flo laughed and wrapped her arms around his neck, pulling him down to her so she could kiss him again. "Yes. That was most definitely a yes."

"I love you, Flo Chiu. You brought me back to life. You reminded me that life was worth living. I wanted to bring you up to the top of a mountain, in a place that was new to both of us, a halfway point for both of us, a place that would just be ours, and ask you to be my wife."

Now the tears fell down her cheeks. She'd been so guarded all her life, never showing her fear or any of her emotions. She hadn't wanted her parents to worry and she hadn't wanted to be looked at like she was weak, so she'd guarded her heart until the day that helicopter had landed on the top of The Hollywood Hills Clinic and changed her life forever.

Since then, it was hard for her to lock those emotions away.

She didn't want to lock that piece of her away.

She looked down at her ring, sparkling in the bright morning sunlight at the top of the world, or at least the highest she'd ever been, and she couldn't believe what a year it had been. Full of changes, full of opportunity, and even though her future was still a bit uncertain, she knew that she had the strongest man at her side. Her rock.

"Well, at least my suspicions about you were well founded."

"How's that?" Nate asked.

"I knew you were up to something. I just never expected this."

"Well," he said, pulling her tight against him, "it was risky. I mean, your dad did lecture me for a long time about wanting to marry his little girl. I also had to put up with your sister and brother. Thankfully your mother and *nainai* were easy on me."

"Yet you still took a chance on me."

He nodded. "You're a risk I'm willing to take, because you're the surest thing in my life and no matter what the future holds for us, I want us to be together forever."

"I feel the same. Though you might change your mind in a few months' time."

He frowned. "What're you talking about?"

"Wedding preparations. My mom told me horror stories about trying to plan her wedding with Dad. Do you really want to even attempt that? I mean, my grandmother in Atlanta is just as stubborn as my *nainai* and when you put the two of them together..." Flo shuddered. "Your mom is so nice. I think she might get eaten alive."

Nate laughed out loud. "How about neither?"

Flo was intrigued. "What are you proposing now?"

"A trip to Vegas after Jasper and eloping."

Flo laughed out loud. "I love it and I'm totally in.

Though you've probably just ruined your relationship with my parents and grandmothers."

"It was your *nainai*'s suggestion, actually."

Flo chuckled. "When do we leave for Vegas?"

"Tomorrow. I have it all arranged."

"You were so certain that I was going to say yes, then?" she teased.

"Yes, it was a risk I was willing to take."

* * * * *

Look out for the next great story in
THE HOLLYWOOD HILLS CLINIC
THE PRINCE AND THE MIDWIFE by Robin Gianna
Available June 2016.

And if you missed where it all started, check out

SEDUCED BY THE HEART SURGEON
by Carol Marinelli
FALLING FOR THE SINGLE DAD
by Emily Forbes
TEMPTED BY HOLLYWOOD'S TOP DOC
by Louisa George

All available now!

MILLS & BOON®
Hardback – May 2016

ROMANCE

Morelli's Mistress	Anne Mather
A Tycoon to Be Reckoned With	Julia James
Billionaire Without a Past	Carol Marinelli
The Shock Cassano Baby	Andie Brock
The Most Scandalous Ravensdale	Melanie Milburne
The Sheikh's Last Mistress	Rachael Thomas
Claiming the Royal Innocent	Jennifer Hayward
Kept at the Argentine's Command	Lucy Ellis
The Billionaire Who Saw Her Beauty	Rebecca Winters
In the Boss's Castle	Jessica Gilmore
One Week with the French Tycoon	Christy McKellen
Rafael's Contract Bride	Nina Milne
Tempted by Hollywood's Top Doc	Louisa George
Perfect Rivals...	Amy Ruttan
English Rose in the Outback	Lucy Clark
A Family for Chloe	Lucy Clark
The Doctor's Baby Secret	Scarlet Wilson
Married for the Boss's Baby	Susan Carlisle
Twins for the Texan	Charlene Sands
Secret Baby Scandal	Joanne Rock

MILLS & BOON®
Large Print – May 2016

ROMANCE

The Queen's New Year Secret	Maisey Yates
Wearing the De Angelis Ring	Cathy Williams
The Cost of the Forbidden	Carol Marinelli
Mistress of His Revenge	Chantelle Shaw
Theseus Discovers His Heir	Michelle Smart
The Marriage He Must Keep	Dani Collins
Awakening the Ravensdale Heiress	Melanie Milburne
His Princess of Convenience	Rebecca Winters
Holiday with the Millionaire	Scarlet Wilson
The Husband She'd Never Met	Barbara Hannay
Unlocking Her Boss's Heart	Christy McKellen

HISTORICAL

In Debt to the Earl	Elizabeth Rolls
Rake Most Likely to Seduce	Bronwyn Scott
The Captain and His Innocent	Lucy Ashford
Scoundrel of Dunborough	Margaret Moore
One Night with the Viking	Harper St. George

MEDICAL

A Touch of Christmas Magic	Scarlet Wilson
Her Christmas Baby Bump	Robin Gianna
Winter Wedding in Vegas	Janice Lynn
One Night Before Christmas	Susan Carlisle
A December to Remember	Sue MacKay
A Father This Christmas?	Louisa Heaton

0416 GEN STD LP

MILLS & BOON®
Hardback – June 2016

ROMANCE

Bought for the Greek's Revenge	Lynne Graham
An Heir to Make a Marriage	Abby Green
The Greek's Nine-Month Redemption	Maisey Yates
Expecting a Royal Scandal	Caitlin Crews
Return of the Untamed Billionaire	Carol Marinelli
Signed Over to Santino	Maya Blake
Wedded, Bedded, Betrayed	Michelle Smart
The Surprise Conti Child	Tara Pammi
The Greek's Nine-Month Surprise	Jennifer Faye
A Baby to Save Their Marriage	Scarlet Wilson
Stranded with Her Rescuer	Nikki Logan
Expecting the Fellani Heir	Lucy Gordon
The Prince and the Midwife	Robin Gianna
His Pregnant Sleeping Beauty	Lynne Marshall
One Night, Twin Consequences	Annie O'Neil
Twin Surprise for the Single Doc	Susanne Hampton
The Doctor's Forbidden Fling	Karin Baine
The Army Doc's Secret Wife	Charlotte Hawkes
A Pregnancy Scandal	Kat Cantrell
A Bride for the Boss	Maureen Child

MILLS & BOON®
Large Print – June 2016

ROMANCE

Leonetti's Housekeeper Bride	Lynne Graham
The Surprise De Angelis Baby	Cathy Williams
Castelli's Virgin Widow	Caitlin Crews
The Consequence He Must Claim	Dani Collins
Helios Crowns His Mistress	Michelle Smart
Illicit Night with the Greek	Susanna Carr
The Sheikh's Pregnant Prisoner	Tara Pammi
Saved by the CEO	Barbara Wallace
Pregnant with a Royal Baby!	Susan Meier
A Deal to Mend Their Marriage	Michelle Douglas
Swept into the Rich Man's World	Katrina Cudmore

HISTORICAL

Marriage Made in Rebellion	Sophia James
A Too Convenient Marriage	Georgie Lee
Redemption of the Rake	Elizabeth Beacon
Saving Marina	Lauri Robinson
The Notorious Countess	Liz Tyner

MEDICAL

Playboy Doc's Mistletoe Kiss	Tina Beckett
Her Doctor's Christmas Proposal	Louisa George
From Christmas to Forever?	Marion Lennox
A Mummy to Make Christmas	Susanne Hampton
Miracle Under the Mistletoe	Jennifer Taylor
His Christmas Bride-to-Be	Abigail Gordon

0516 GEN STD LP

MILLS & BOON®

Why shop at millsandboon.co.uk?

Each year, thousands of romance readers find their perfect read at millsandboon.co.uk. That's because we're passionate about bringing you the very best romantic fiction. Here are some of the advantages of shopping at www.millsandboon.co.uk:

* **Get new books first**—you'll be able to buy your favourite books one month before they hit the shops

* **Get exclusive discounts**—you'll also be able to buy our specially created monthly collections, with up to 50% off the RRP

* **Find your favourite authors**—latest news, interviews and new releases for all your favourite authors and series on our website, plus ideas for what to try next

* **Join in**—once you've bought your favourite books, don't forget to register with us to rate, review and join in the discussions

Visit **www.millsandboon.co.uk**
for all this and more today!

MA
McL